THE TOWER

Human minds were molded by the spiders. They were the undisputed masters of their human slaves. But what they had not anticipated was that another human mind might take advantage of their training and achieve direct control of their slaves.

Now, Niall was suddenly aware of why the Death Lord was so anxious to uncover his secret. If human beings could master the techniques of mind control, then the days of spider supremacy were over . . .

SPIDER WORLD

It's *their* planet now . . . or is it?

COLIN WILSON

Colin Wilson is the author of more than fifty novels, plays and essays. His first book, *The Outsider*, was greeted with extraordinary critical acclaim. His work covers a wide spectrum of topics—from philosophy to mysticism, from the criminal to the psychic—and includes *The Occult, The Psychic Detectives* and *Poltergeists!*, as well as the science fiction classics *The Mind Parasites* and *Lifeforce*.

Ace Books by Colin Wilson

THE SPIDER WORLD TRILOGY

THE DESERT
THE TOWER
THE FORTRESS
(coming in July)

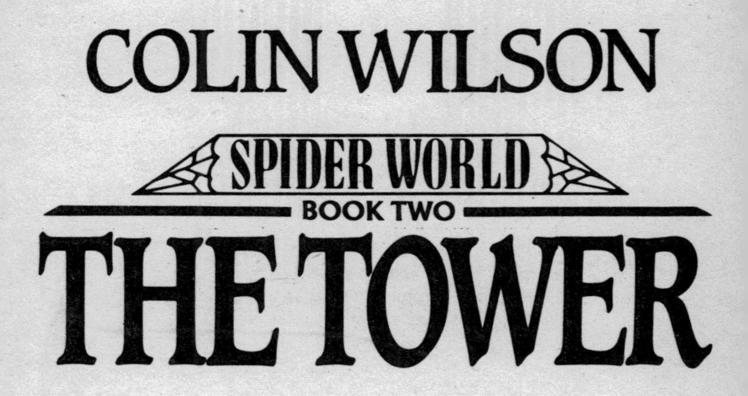

ACE BOOKS, NEW YORK

This Ace Book contains the complete
text of the original edition.
It has been completely reset in a typeface
designed for easy reading, and was printed
from new film.

SPIDER WORLD: THE TOWER

An Ace Book/published by arrangement with
the author

PRINTING HISTORY
Grafton edition published 1987
Ace edition/January 1989

Cover art by Louis Rey.

For information address: The Berkley Publishing Group,
200 Madison Avenue, New York, New York 10016.

ISBN: 0-441-77811-9

Ace Books are published by The Berkley Publishing Group,
200 Madison Avenue, New York, New York 10016.

PRINTED IN THE UNITED STATES OF AMERICA

10 9 8 7 6 5 4 3 2 1

ACKNOWLEDGMENTS

My chief debt of gratitude is to my friend Donald Seaman, with whom this book was originally planned as a collaboration. The idea was abandoned at a fairly early stage, but I had the benefit of his suggestions and advice throughout. I am also deeply grateful to Professor John Cloudsley-Thompson, England's leading expert on deserts, for his invaluable advice on the first section of this book. It also owed a great deal to the warm encouragement of my editor John Boothe.

CW
Cornwall, 1986

For Sally, Damon and Rowan

It was fortunate for Niall that he encountered no predators that afternoon. He was in a state of shock, and rebellion against fate. He felt that he had been pushed too far, his emotional resources drained dry. If a scorpion or tiger beetle had blocked his path, he would have stared at it with a kind of bored disgust, as if it had somehow come too late. It was pleasant, but a little frightening, to be totally without fear.

He moved fast, following the marks in the sand. The spiders were so light footed that they left little sign of their passage; it was impossible to guess how many there were. The footprints of Veig and Siris were quite clear; from their depth in the soft sand, he could tell that they were carrying burdens—probably Runa and Mara. Yet although he continually strained his eyes towards the horizon, he caught no glimpse of them.

The route lay along the western edge of the rocky wilderness between the burrow and the country of the ants.

The main vegetation was thorn and tamarisk; the sand was strewn with black volcanic pebbles. The countryside rose gradually to a range of mountains in the distance; to the east lay the black peaks of spent volcanoes. It was a bare and inhospitable country, and the westerly wind, that had blown over miles of hot grey rock, dried the sweat as fast as it formed on his body. He took pleasure in his feeling of grim indifference to these discomforts. The thought of Ulf's bloated corpse made him feel that physical pain was a boring triviality.

He had lost all sense of time, and was mildly surprised to notice that the sun was not far above the western horizon. The hills were now closer. The earth underfoot was red in colour, and there were red rocks stretching into the distance, some of them tall pillars more than a hundred feet high. It was time to look for a place to sleep. But in this bleak land, no spot seemed preferable to any other. Eventually, he came upon a great slab of red stone, buried in the earth at an angle of about thirty degrees. A thorn bush had grown in its shelter. Niall spent half an hour hacking it out of the ground, then smoothing the place where it had grown. Then he ate his evening meal—dried meat and cactus fruit. The taste of the bitter spring water from the depths of the burrow brought a feeling of nostalgia, and a sudden desire to burst into tears. He fought it back, clenching his teeth, and began gathering rocks to make his shelter impregnable to night predators. In this barren land it seemed an unnecessary precaution, but the activity helped him to suppress the increasing feeling of sorrow forcing its way through the numbness.

In the early hours of the morning, he was glad of his precaution. He was awakened by the sound of movement on the other side of the thorn bush. There was now a faint moon, and he could see the outline of some large creature, probably a scorpion. It had detected his presence, perhaps by some involuntary movement in his sleep. His hand reached out and gripped the metal cylinder. He could hear the scraping noise of the creature's armoured body on the stones. Then the thorn bush moved. He gripped the nearest branch in both hands, and resisted the pull. Aware of this resistance, the creature began to circle the bush, looking for a point of access. Niall forced himself into a half-sitting position, his head pressed against the sloping rock above; hearing his movements, the creature redoubled its efforts. The moon was reflected briefly from a multifaceted eye. It was attempting to force a gap between the piled rocks and the top of the thorn bush, using its armoured shoulders as a wedge. Niall felt the light touch of a feeler against his foot. Leaning forward, he pressed hard on the side of the cylinder; with a click, it slid open; at the same time, Niall jabbed with all his strength. There was a hiss of pain, and the thorn bush was pulled several feet. Expecting at any moment to feel jaws closing on his flesh, Niall again jabbed into the darkness with his spear. It connected again, sinking into something soft. Then the creature turned, and he saw the glint of moonlight on its scaly back as it scuttled off. Whatever it was, it had decided that its intended prey had a dangerous sting. Niall dragged the bush back into position, then lay down again, the spear beside him. When he opened his eyes again, it was dawn. He lay and watched the sun rise, shivering in the chilly air, then ate some dried meat, washed it down with water, and set off once more towards the hills.

As the ground rose, the air was cooler; the atmosphere was warm and hazy. Although the ground was too hard to show traces of footprints, he was certain that his family had already passed this way; the worn, overgrown track had once been an ancient road, and was the obvious route to the main pass across the hills. In one place where it descended into a narrow valley, dust had accumulated, and he could once again discern clearly the footprints of Siris and Veig, and the lighter marks made by the spiders.

A few miles farther on, he came upon a cistern by the side of the road. It had been made of large slabs of granite, evidently transported from elsewhere; it was about two feet wide, its top half covered with a large, flat stone. The water was very clear, and there was green lichen clinging to the walls below the surface. Niall took his cup from his pack—it had been carved out of wood by Jomar—and dipped it into the water; it was startlingly cold. After drinking his fill, Niall poured water over his head and shoulders, laughing aloud with relief and delight as the cold water made channels through the dust on his skin.

There were also clear signs that his mother and brother had halted there; he recognised the mark of a sandal they had brought as a present from Sefna to her sister. Yet although he searched the ground minutely, he could find no sign of the footprints of the children.

As he stared into the water, and at the moss-covered stones that had fallen into it, he experienced a glow of awakening energy, immediately extinguished by the thought of his dead father. But it was the first time in two days that he had felt that spontaneous upsurge of pure joy in being alive. He stared into the water, allowing his mind to relax as if sinking into the cool depths, with their green-shaded lights. He felt as if he were relaxing into a comfortable bed; yet his mind remained as wide awake as ever. Part of his consciousness was aware of his wet hair, of the sun beating down on his back, of the hardness of the ground against his knees; another part was floating in the shadowy coolness, drifting peacefully as if time had come to a stop.

Then, suddenly, the water had disappeared, and he was looking at his brother Veig. Veig was lying on his back, his eyes closed, his head propped against the roots of a tree. He was obviously exhausted, for his mouth hung open and his face looked grey and lifeless. But he was not dead, for his chest was heaving. Perched close to his head, a few inches away, was the pepsis wasp. It seemed to be guarding him in his sleep.

His mother was seated nearby, drinking water in tiny sips from a gourd. She also looked tired, and her face was covered with black streaks where perspiration had mixed with the dust of travel.

Without being aware of how he knew it, Niall realised that this scene was taking place at this moment. He noted there was no sign of the two children, and that the four spiders who were stretched out in the sunlight were brown and not black. By merely transferring his attention, he was able to examine them as carefully as if he were standing beside them. Their bodies were covered with brown, velvety hair. Their faces, seen from in front, looked oddly human, for they had two enormous black eyes under a kind of forehead. Under these there was a curved row of smaller eyes; and under these, a protuberance that looked like a flat nose. The chelicerae with their folded fangs resembled a beard. Both the front legs and the chelicerae looked very powerful. The abdominal section was smaller and slimmer than in most spiders. When one of them heaved itself to its feet to turn its face into the glare of the sun, it conveyed an impression of muscular strength and athleticism. These creatures actually seemed to enjoy the sunlight.

Niall had never seen a wolf spider before, but it was obvious to him that these were hunting spiders, who captured their prey by sheer speed. He also observed that there were two more large, black eyes at the back of the head, giving them all round vision.

The countryside around them was not unlike the country of the ants: a green plain with trees and bushes; he could see red berries on the nearest bush. There were also palm trees and tall cedars. But his vision was limited to the area in the immediate vicinity of the spiders.

Niall was also interested to observe that he was aware of what was taking place in the minds of the drowsing wolf spiders. Because they hunted their prey, rather than waiting for it to blunder into a trap, their mental outlook seemed closer to that of human beings rather than to that of web-building spiders, and their thought processes were somehow active rather than passive. This velvet-brown spider whose face was now receiving the force of the midday sun was thinking about how many days it would take to get back home again. Niall tried to grasp what it meant by "home," and glimpsed a bewildering picture of an immense city full of towers—incredible square towers, full of windows. Between these towers stretched spider webs, their strands as thick as his grass rope. And in one of these strange towers lurked a being whose name filled everyone with fear. When Niall tried to grasp the source of this fear, he seemed to find himself in a vast, dark hall across which stretched hundreds of grey cobwebs. And from somewhere in its darkest corner, down a tunnel of cobwebs, black eyes were watching him with the cold curiosity of a death spider.

Now, suddenly, Niall began to experience a disquietude that made his flesh crawl. Until this moment, he had felt himself a detached observer, bodiless and therefore invulnerable. Now, staring into the eyes that watched him from among the cobwebs, he felt for the first time as if he were actually there in the dark hall, being studied by a totally merciless intelligence. As the disquietude hardened into dread, Niall instinctively closed his eyes; the vision immediately vanished, and he found himself looking once more into the clear water of the cistern, and at the slimy green moss that had grown on its sides.

He looked round nervously, and was relieved to find himself alone. In spite of the heat of the day, his body felt icy cold. And although he was now back in the country of barren red sandstone, he continued to feel that the black eyes were watching him from amid the tangle of cobwebs. It took several minutes for this impression to fade.

As his skin began to absorb the sun's heat, he realised with surprise that he was hungry. In the stress and misery of the past two days he had felt little or no desire for food. Now his appetite was back again. He ate slowly, crunching some of the dry, biscuitlike bread they had brought from Dira, and enjoying the luxury of washing it down with draughts of cold water.

When he had refilled the gourd with spring water, he relaxed in the shade of a thorn tree—first jabbing between the roots with his spear to make sure there were no centipedes. Lying there, staring at the milky blue sky through the branches, he became aware that his natural optimism had returned with his appetite. It was plain to him now that, since his father's death, a cloud had descended on his mind and turned him into a sleepwalker. Now it was as if he was awake again, and his powers of reason had begun to reassert themselves.

Ever since he had left the burrow, his energies had been directed to a single purpose: to join his family. Without thinking about it clearly, he had accepted that this would involve allowing himself to become a captive of the spiders.

But then he had made the natural assumption that his family were in the hands of the death spiders. Now he knew this was not so, the situation looked altogether less hopeless. If he allowed himself to be taken prisoner, the brown hunting spiders would be in a position to watch his every movement. But while he was free, he could watch them—and watch for an opportunity to free his family . . .

Before he could do that, he had to catch up with them. Reluctantly—for his body still ached with tiredness—he heaved himself to his feet, pulled on his pack and resumed the climb to the top of the pass.

The road wound upward between columns of weather-worn sandstone, which in places lay across the road as if hurled there by an earthquake. The higher he climbed, the steeper the path became. From this height, he could look back on the route he had travelled; on the far horizon lay the great plateau, surrounded by desert. He seemed to be the only creature alive in this immense, empty landscape. For a long time he stared at it—the land in which his whole life had so far been spent. Then he turned and forced his aching legs to climb the last thousand feet to the summit.

Suddenly he felt the breeze blowing cool against the sweat on his body; it was being channelled between high sandstone cliffs, and it carried a smell that he had never encountered before—a sharp, clean scent that made his heart lift. Ten minutes later, he was looking down on a strip of green plain, beyond which lay the immense expanse of the sea. Even at this distance, the strong, sharp wind carried the smell of salt spray. An enormous exultation made his heart expand. He felt that he was looking at a land that he had known in the remote past, at a time long before spiders were lords of the earth.

It was already late afternoon; if he wanted to reach the plain before dusk, he would have to start now. He raised the gourd to his mouth, to moisten his throat before beginning the long descent. As he did so, a voice in his ear said clearly: "Niall, be careful."

The shock almost made him drop the gourd; the water he was drinking went down the wrong way and made him choke. He had expected to see his mother standing behind him; but there was no one. Neither was there any cover where someone could hide. He was standing in the middle of the road, the sheer cliffs rising on either side.

He felt so shaken that he sat down on the nearest rock. It was only then, trying to reconstruct the sensation, that he decided that the voice had not spoken in his ear, but inside his head.

He stared down at the flat green plain below, with its trees and bushes. He could see no sign of living creatures. Yet somewhere down there, Siris was watching him. She must have seen him outlined against the skyline. And if she had been watching for him, he could be certain that the brown hunting spiders had also been watching.

As he gazed at the plain, trying to guess where the hidden eyes were concealed, her voice spoke again. "Go back. Go back." This time it was undoubtedly inside his chest, and it seemed to be an impulse rather than a verbal message.

He looked behind him, over the path he had travelled, and knew it was pointless to tell him to go back. There was nowhere to go. He might succeed in hiding in a cave or gulley for a few hours. But discovery would be inevitable. This bare landscape offered no concealment.

He was left with two choices: to stay where he was, or to go forward. He chose without hesitation. It was better to act than to do nothing. He swung the pannier onto his shoulders, and started on the long downhill road to the plain.

As soon as he began to move, he felt surprisingly light hearted. Niall was too young and inexperienced to know real fear. Faced with the same choice, his father or grandfather would unhesitatingly have chosen flight and concealment—not out of fear, but out of recognition that a man who allowed himself to fall into the hands of the spiders had virtually condemned himself to life imprisonment. It was Niall's ignorance that enabled him to march towards captivity without deep misgivings. Because the future was unknown, it seemed full of promise.

The downhill road was straighter, and therefore steeper, than the southern approach to the pass; it made the calves of his legs ache. As he descended towards the plain, the sea disappeared beyond the horizon, and some of the lightness went out of his heart. But he was excited at the thought of seeing his mother and brother again, and strained his eyes continually for any sign of movement on the green expanse below. There were many locations where the spiders might have lain in concealment, and as he approached such places, his heart contracted with tension. But when, after two hours, the road became less steep, and the nearest trees were only a few hundred yards ahead, he began to wonder if he was mistaken to believe the spiders knew of his presence. The thought brought a twinge of disappointment. Now there were no large rocks ahead, not even a bush that was large enough to conceal a grasshopper.

This thought was passing through his mind as his eye caught a blur of movement at the edge of his vision. Then he was hurled forward on to the ground with such force that the breath was knocked from his body. Powerful forelegs seized him and turned him over; his arms pressed to his sides, he was lifted clear of the ground. He screamed as he found himself looking into black, featureless eyes, while unfolded fangs were raised to strike. Instinctively, he froze, hoping to disarm the aggression by immobility. Then claws seized him from behind; he felt the pannier removed from his back, and a loop of sticky silk passed around his body, pinioning his arms.

When the first shock had passed, he became oddly calm.

It may have been the humanoid look of the faces that reassured him. They might have been intelligent lobsters, with the faces of old men. At close quarters, the hunting spiders had a peculiar, musky smell which was not unpleasant. When unfolded, their fangs were terrifying; but when folded into the chelicerae, they looked not unlike two elaborately curled bunches of hair at the end of a beard. After those first few terrifying seconds, when Niall expected to be injected with poison, he understood that they had no intention of harming him, and allowed them to see, by his passivity, that he had no intention of trying to escape.

The spider that held him raised his body clear of the ground so the other spider could tie his ankles. Whilst moist, the silk had an elastic, pliable quality; yet although scarcely thicker than a blade of marram grass, it seemed virtually unbreakable. Niall's ankles felt glued together.

When his arms and legs had been secured, Niall was swung over onto the spider's back, and held there by its pedipalps—the nearest thing a spider possesses to a pair of arms—and then, suddenly, they were in motion, flying over the hard ground at a speed that made his head whirl. The spider ran with a loping motion, so Niall bounced up and down with every long stride. When, periodically, he seemed about to fall sideways off the velvety back, the spider reached up with its forelegs, without breaking its stride, and readjusted his position. Behind them ran the other wolf spider, carrying Niall's pack.

Niall had often seen the camel spider—or solifugid—travelling across the desert at this speed, looking like a ball of windblown grass; he had never expected to look down on the ground as it flashed past his eyes at fifty miles an hour. He tried turning his head sideways and focusing his eyes on the horizon; this made him feel less dizzy, but the bumping of his head against the spider's back made it impossible to keep his gaze fixed for more than a few moments at a time. Finally he closed his eyes, gritting his teeth, and concentrated on enduring the jerky motion that made the blood roar in his ears.

Then, quite suddenly, he was lying on the ground, and there was a face looking down at him. A moment later, he recognised the familiar smell of his mother's hair as she held him tight against her and kissed his face. Then Veig helped him into a sitting position and held a cup of water to his lips. His mouth felt dry, and his throat was full of dust, so he coughed violently when he tried to swallow. He realised that his hands and legs were now free, although the skin was torn where the sticky web had been pulled away.

His senses cleared; he realised he must have fainted. The spider on whose back he had travelled—the largest of the four, and obviously the leader—was standing there, looking at him with its featureless black eyes; the line between its mouth and the folded chelicerae looked like a pair of downturned lips, pursed in disapproval, while the row of smaller eyes below the main ones looked like some curious disfigurement, a row of shiny, black warts. It was not even breathing heavily.

Veig said: "Do you feel strong enough to walk?"

"I think so." He stood up unsteadily. Siris began to cry.

"They say we have to move on," Veig said.

The contents of his pack, he saw, had been emptied out on the ground, and one of the spiders was examining them one by one, prodding them with its foreleg or with a pedipalp. It picked up the metal tube, looked at it briefly, and tossed it down among the prickly pears and dried bread. At the same time, Niall felt the mind of the big spider probing his own. It was trying to observe his reaction to this search of his belongings. But its insight was crude and uncomprehending. It probed his mind as clumsily as the other spider was examining the contents of his pack, as if prodding with a blunt finger.

Then its attention was distracted; the other spider was looking with interest at the folded sheet of spider silk Niall used as a sleeping bag. The big spider went and examined it carefully, and Niall could feel the impulses of communication that passed between them. Their language was not verbal; it consisted of a series of feelings and intuitions. Neither of them could say: "I wonder where this came from?" but what passed between them was a questioning impulse, accompanied by an image of the death spider that had vanished in the desert. Simultaneously—their minds seemed to work in concert—both spiders recognised that this silk was too old to be the death spider's balloon, and they immediately lost interest in it.

Suddenly both spiders became alert. Niall could see no obvious reason for this sudden vigilance. The big spider hurried off to a nearby thorn tree. When Niall looked more closely, he could see that they had spun a web between the lower branches and the trunk. A big grasshopper had jumped straight into it and was struggling frantically. It made no sound—the spiders in any case were deaf—but the vibrations of its panic had instantly communicated themselves.

While they watched, the big spider paralysed the grasshopper with one swift jab of its fang, detached it from the web by biting through its strands, then proceeded to eat it. It was obviously hungry.

Niall took the opportunity to ask the question that had been constantly on his mind. "Where are Runa and Mara?"

"They took them off in balloons."

"And the wasp and the ants?"

Veig nodded towards the spiders. "Inside them," he said drily.

A moment later, a violent blow knocked him forward on his face. One of the spiders was standing over him, its fangs extended ready to strike. When Veig tried to sit up, it pushed him down again with a blow of its powerful foreleg. Veig lay passively, looking up at the exposed fang that hovered threateningly over his face. Once again, Niall felt his own mind probed by the leader, which had now finished its meal. It wanted to gauge his reaction to the threat to his brother. Niall was glad that his chief emotion was anxiety; he felt instinctively that any sign of anger or aggression would have been punished instantly.

When it had made its point—that talking was not allowed—the spider moved away and allowed Veig to sit up. Then it prodded Niall with its pedipalp and indicated the contents of his pack; it was clearly an order to replace them. As Niall did this, he again felt the mind of the leader probing his own. He observed with satisfaction that he was able to keep his mind empty and passive, and that the spider seemed satisfied.

Five minutes later they were on the move again. Siris looked weary and drained of emotion. Niall could sense that she was still in a state of shock at the death of her husband, and separation from the girls. He could also sense that her delight in seeing him again was neutralised by a feeling of despair that he was now a prisoner. She seemed to feel guilty, as if this was her fault. Niall longed to talk to her; but under the continual surveillance of the spiders, this was impossible.

The spiders moved fast, and they expected their prisoners to keep up with them. Now, at last, Niall could understand how they had covered so much ground. For them, human walking speed was an unbearably slow crawl. So the prisoners were forced to move at a trot, while the spiders marched alongside at what was, for them, a leisurely walking pace. At first Niall was hampered by the pack on his back, which bounced up and down. When the leader noticed this, it took it from him, and one of the others was made to carry it. It was a relief to be free of the burden.

With more leisure for observation, Niall would have enjoyed the countryside through which they were now passing. He had never seen anywhere so green. This fertile coastal plain had once been rich farmland—they passed more than one half-ruined farmhouse—and had now been allowed to return to its natural state, with many varieties of trees and tangled grass underfoot. Insects hummed past them—flies, wasps, dragonflies—and grasshoppers chirped in the undergrowth. To Niall it appeared a kind of paradise, and it seemed ironic that he should be seeing it for the first time as a prisoner.

An hour later, with the sun sinking behind the mountains, they halted for the night. The humans were all exhausted; they flung themselves on the ground, their faces turned to the sky, breathing deeply. One of the spiders began to spin a web under the nearest low tree, while the others basked in the evening sunlight. As the pounding of Niall's heart subsided, he drifted off into a pleasant state of relaxation. Momentarily, he felt the mind of the leader probe his own; but it was obviously a matter of routine, and he could sense its lack of interest. In a semi-dreamlike state, he tuned in to the minds of the spiders. It was rather like overhearing their conversation, except that he was also aware of their physical sensations. At the moment their chief concern was hunger. Spiders, he now realised, ate only living food, so could not carry their rations with them when they were travelling. It was not simply that they preferred the taste of fresh meat; there was something else—something about the life-force itself—that they enjoyed and absorbed.

It also became clear to Niall that, compared to human beings, these creatures were almost entirely the slaves of instinct. For millions of years they had been little more than food-catching machines whose whole lives centred on seizing their prey and injecting it with venom. They had no other interest in life. Niall could enjoy the scenery and think about distant places, use his imagination. The wolf spiders were indifferent to the scenery, except as a possible source of food, and totally lacked anything that might be called imagination.

Fortunately, they were surrounded by an abundance of food. Before the light had faded, the web had caught half a dozen meat flies, two wasps and a butterfly, and these had immediately been paralysed and handed to the spiders in order of rank. As they ate their living prey, their minds became a glow of immense satisfaction. Niall realised with alarm that part of their hostility towards human beings was that they regarded them as potential food; when they were hungry, it seemed a waste to be escorting these prisoners instead of eating them. But as soon as they had satisfied their appetite, this irritability disappeared. They made no attempt to prevent the prisoners from gathering fruit from the bushes, and watched with tolerance as Niall climbed a coconut palm and tossed down the green coconuts into Veig's waiting hands. The humans found the slightly astringent milk deliciously refreshing, ideal for washing down the dried rodent flesh and stale bread. With a good meal inside them, their spirits began to revive. A curious atmosphere of mutual tolerance built up between the humans and the spiders. Niall became aware that these huge, immensely powerful creatures were the slaves of the death spiders; their attitude towards their masters was one of respect, but with an undertone of fear and resentment. They disliked obeying orders and would have preferred to be free to lie in the sun and catch insects. Even web-building was not natural to them. They did it because it was the simplest way of catching food; but their natural inclination was to catch their prey with swiftness and strength. Hunting gave them the deepest satisfaction they knew.

He was so tired that he slept that night without covering, on a makeshift bed of grass and leaves. When he opened his eyes again it was dawn, and one of the spiders was already devouring a flying beetle that had been caught in the web. The other spiders were dozing in the sun; unlike the death spiders, these hunters had no love for the hours of darkness, and the return of daylight filled them with a drowsy satisfaction. Observing their lazy, slow-moving minds, Niall was reminded of the ants. It filled him with a peculiar excitement, this ability to understand the minds of his captors. All his life, he had been terrified of the spiders. Now some deep intuition told him that this conquest of fear was the beginning of a far greater conquest.

They ate a breakfast of fruit and dried meat, washed down again with the milk of the green coconut. The spiders had by this time eaten their fill—as the sun rose, an abundance of flying insects blundered into their web. When he came close to this web, Niall observed that it had a pleasant, sweetish smell; this was obviously what attracted the insects.

Veig whispered: "I wonder what we're waiting for?"

Niall said: "They're waiting . . ." He hesitated, unable to finish the sentence.

"I *know* that. But what for?"

"For . . . for someone. For . . . people."

Veig and Siris both looked at him curiously.

"How did you know that?"

Niall shrugged and shook his head. It was a subject he was not willing to discuss in front of the spiders.

Half an hour went by. The sun was hot, but there was a pleasant breeze from the north. The humans moved into the shade of a thorn tree, while the spiders continued to doze in the sun; they seemed to be able to absorb a degree of heat that would have given a human being sunstroke. One of them rolled on its back, exposing its grey, soft underbelly to the warmth. The spiders were so confident of their ability to read the minds of human beings that they felt no need to take precautions.

Niall decided to try an experiment. He was curious to know how far the spiders would respond to purely mental danger signals. He imagined taking the metal tube out of his pannier, making it expand into a spear, and driving it into the spider's exposed belly. The spider showed no reaction. Next, Niall imagined picking up a large, flat stone that lay nearby, and bringing it down with all his strength on the head of the dozing spider. Once again, there was no reaction. He was aware that this was because he was merely toying with the idea, with no intention of putting it into practice. So he deliberately made a powerful effort of imagination, and tried to envisage what it would be like to stroll over to the flat stone, then to raise it above his head and dash it down on the upturned belly. This time, the spider became uncomfortable; it moved its head so its eyes could see in all directions, and rolled over onto its stomach. It glanced suspiciously at the human beings, and Niall felt the clumsy probe of its mind. He relaxed his own mind into drowsy immobility, deliberately creating a mental wave-length of a tent spider. The spider's vigilance relaxed, and after a few seconds, its mind again fell into the soothing, repetitive rhythm of physical pleasure.

Then, suddenly, the leader became alert; it sprang to its

feet—Niall again had an opportunity to observe the swiftness of its reactions—and stared intently towards the north. Niall listened, but could hear nothing but the normal sounds of the morning. It was at least another minute before he was able to detect the sound of movement in the bushes. Again, he marvelled at the acuteness of the spider's senses.

A moment later, he was amazed to see the figure of a man emerging from among the trees. At the same instant, the reaction of the spiders told him that this was what they had been waiting for.

The man who now marched confidently towards them was a magnificent specimen, well over six feet tall, with powerful shoulders and a deep chest. He wore a woven tunic, and his shoulder-length blond hair was held round his head with a circlet of metal. For a brief moment, Niall thought he was looking at Hamna, then, as the man came closer, knew he was a stranger.

Ten feet away, the man came to a halt, fell on one knee, and made a gesture of obeisance to the spiders. The leader sent out a brusque impulse of acknowledgement that also contained an element of impatience, as if to ask: "Where have you been?" The man's attitude expressed total subservience. The spider transmitted a mental order that signified: "Very well, let's go," and the man again inclined his head.

Niall expected the newcomer to greet them, or at least, to exchange a glance of sympathy. In fact, he ignored them. In response to a gesture from the leader, he picked up Niall's pannier and slung it on his back, then stood there, waiting for the next order. Niall studied his face with interest. The eyes were mild and blue, and there was a hint of weakness in the downturned mouth and unassertive chin. He moved with a precision that Niall at first took to be self-assurance, but which he soon recognised as the indifference of a well-trained animal.

When Siris stood up, and used a short length of grass-rope to tie back her long hair, the man eyed her with momentary interest. But it lasted only a fraction of a second. Then he looked back at the spiders, waiting for orders. It was obvious that he felt no fellow-feeling for the captives.

The big spider gave the order to march, and the man set off towards the north, walking with long, swift strides. Niall, Siris and Veig were made to follow, all three obliged to break into a trot to keep up with the newcomer. The spiders walked behind at their own leisurely pace; Niall could sense their relief that the main part of their journey was over.

Once he had established that the spiders were communicating amongst themselves, Niall tried to tune in to the mind of the man in front. He found it a frustrating exercise. His mind seemed as blank and indifferent as that of a grey desert spider. But, unlike the desert spiders, he seemed totally unaware that Niall was trying to probe his thoughts and feelings. This was not because his mind was attentive and vigilant, but because his attention was directed solely at the outside world. He was indifferent to everything else.

Because the newcomer set the pace, the journey was less exhausting than on the previous day. They were refreshed after a good night's sleep, and the cool breeze was pleasant. Niall found the smell of sun-warmed vegetation intoxicating. Soon he heard a sound that was new to him: the cry of seagulls. His blood tingled with excitement. And when, ten minutes later, they reached the top of a low rise and looked down on the sea, he experienced a surge of exultation that made him want to laugh aloud. This was quite unlike the salt lake of Thellam. It was a deeper blue, and it stretched as far as the eye could see. Waves crashed onto the beach where three small craft were waiting, and salt spray blew against his face like rain. This great expanse of salt water, with its white-capped waves, seemed the most beautiful thing he had ever seen.

There were people lying on the sand; when the big man shouted, they scrambled hastily to their feet and stood to attention. Then, when they saw the spiders, they all dropped on one knee and made gestures of obeisance. The big man shouted an order, and they again stood to attention. Niall was surprised to realise that there were women among them: strong, big-breasted women with hair even longer than his mother's. They stared straight in front of them, their arms down by their sides, while the breeze whipped their hair round their faces. Even when Niall and Veig stood directly in front of them, their eyes did not waver. Niall, who was totally unacquainted with military discipline, found it bizarre and rather disquieting. These human beings were trying to pretend that they were trees or stones.

The men, he saw, were as well built as their guide, and all had the same muscular arms and thighs. But their faces, while handsome and impressive, somehow lacked individuality. The women—there were three of them—were all beautiful, with slim, strong bodies and well-shaped features. Like the men, they wore no covering on the upper part of their bodies, and their bare breasts were suntanned. Veig surveyed them with incredulous delight, like a hungry man presented with a good meal.

The big man shouted an order in a language Niall found incomprehensible; the men and women broke ranks, and began to haul the ships into the water. Each of these craft was about thirty feet long, and had a curved prow and stern. Once they were afloat, the spiders approached the shoreline and halted within ten feet of the breaking waves. They folded their legs underneath them; then two men approached each one, lifted them, and carried them into the boats, holding them well clear of the waves. After this, the women clambered in, one to each boat. Niall, Veig and Siris were also ordered to separate, one to each craft; Niall found himself sharing a boat with the big spider and one of his subordinates.

These long, graceful vessels were of the type that had once carried Vikings over northern seas, built of overlapping planks, with a deep keel. The centre of the ship broadened, then narrowed again towards the stern, giving it an outline that resembled a swan. In the middle of the boat was a canvas tent, in which the big spider had been housed; its subordinate was in a kind of basket sheltered by the prow. Niall could sense that both were deeply uneasy; travel by sea ran counter to their strongest instincts.

Niall was fascinated by everything about the long ships. To the men who travelled in them, they were cramped and uncomfortable, but for Niall they were miracles of mysterious craftsmanship. They had no decks and—apart from the canvas tent—no shelter. Wooden seats ran along either side, and each side of the ship had seven oar-holes with rowlocks. The central space was reserved for the mast, which was lying flat in the bottom, and for barrels and ropes. Niall was ordered into a seat in the stern. His pack was handed to him. There he sat, trying to be inconspicuous, absorbing everything that went on around him. The men sat facing him on their benches and unshipped their oars. The woman stood on a low wooden platform with a supporting rail, facing the rowers. A man with a long pole pushed out the ship until it was a dozen yards from the shore and well clear of the other two craft. Then, at an order from the woman, the men leaned forward and heaved on their oars. The woman began a rhythmic chant, beating time with her hands; the oarsmen rowed perfectly in time. Niall felt so exhilarated as they surged forward into the waves that he felt like shouting for joy.

Not all the men were rowing; half of them sat on benches between the oars, or strolled up and down the gangway, talking amongst themselves. Niall also stood up and looked over the side, and no one seemed to object. The sight of the waves breaking against the prow of the boat struck him as unutterably beautiful.

Listening carefully to the men, he now realised that they were not speaking some foreign tongue. Their language was recognisably the same as his own, but strangely accented, so he had to strain his attention to understand it. And when the woman shouted orders in the same language, it again became incomprehensible.

The woman, he soon recognised, was the most important person on board. In all the men he sensed an attitude of respect, even of worship. This was understandable—she was tall, and had corn-coloured hair and perfect teeth—but Niall sensed that it was not her beauty they admired so much. When, after half an hour or so, she beckoned one of the men and ordered him to take her place on the platform, he dropped onto one knee and kissed her hand, then remained in that position until she stepped down. As she walked down the central aisle of the boat, the seamen hastened to make way for her. When she snapped her fingers, one of them handed her a garment of some animal skin with which she covered her shoulders. The wind was becoming chilly. A little later, the woman strolled over to Niall—who was now sitting, trying to keep warm—and looked down at him with an expression of mingled curiosity and contempt. He found it easy to read her mind. She was thinking—although without words—"This one won't be of much use." Something in her contemptuous gaze reminded him of the princess Merlew, and the memory of humiliation still made him wince.

The spiders had relapsed into a state of miserable passivity, and the woman seemed to know this. On this boat, she, not the spiders, was the supreme commander. When Niall turned his attention to the big spider in his canvas tent, he was surprised at the depth of its fear and anxiety. It was afloat on an element over which it had no control; every heave or roll of the ship made it feel sick. It was totally indifferent to everything except its nausea and desire to be back on dry land.

When they had been at sea for about two hours, another relay of oarsmen took over; they did this by sitting beside an oarsman and allowed him to slip away, so that not a stroke was lost. The men who had been relieved flung themselves flat in the centre aisle and gave themselves up to the bliss of relaxation; this was so strong that Niall could feel it flowing around him in waves, producing a delicious light-heartedness.

Towards midday, the wind dropped, then changed round to the south-east. The woman shouted an order. The sailors who had been drowsing in the sun leapt to their feet and raised the mast. This fitted into a receptacle made from a hollowed tree trunk. Then a triangular sail was raised. Niall was curious to see how the ship could continue to sail due north when the wind was blowing from the south-east, and was fascinated by the movable boom that allowed the sail to be moved around to catch the wind at the right angle. His ability to read the minds of the sailors made it possible for him to understand exactly what they were doing.

Now the ship was under sail, the oarsmen could relax. Food was served, and Niall was handed a plate. He was very hungry, and the food seemed exquisite—soft white bread, nuts, and a creamy white drink that he had never tasted before—it was, in fact, cow's milk. A man came and sat beside him, and tried to make conversation, but Niall found his accent impossible to follow. When he tried to understand by tuning in to the man's mind, he found this equally frustrating—it seemed to be almost a blank, a mere response to his physical sensations. The man soon gave up and moved off to talk to someone else. Niall was relieved to be left alone. It seemed strange that such magnificent physical specimens should have such oddly feeble minds.

The food made him sleepy, and he lay on the floor and dozed, his head on his pack. But after a pleasant and peaceful sleep, he began to experience a nightmare in which he seemed to be choking and feeling sick. As his senses returned, he became aware that his mind was picking up the acute mental distress of the two spiders. The reason, he soon realised, was that the ship was plunging up and down with increased violence; the wind had risen so that it took three men to control the sail. The sky was full of dark clouds. He stood up and looked over the side. The other two boats were in sight, about half a mile away, and the wind was driving them forward at tremendous speed. But it was also becoming stronger by the moment. A wave suddenly broke over the side of the ship, covering them all with spray. Yet the sailors seemed unconcerned. They had sailed in worse weather than this, and had total confidence in their ship.

When another gust of wind seemed to threaten to turn the ship on its side, the commander ordered the men to lower the sail. Oarsmen again took their places on the benches. At that moment, the rain began to fall; but Niall could hardly distinguish it from the salt spray. He experienced a tremendous feeling of exhilaration, the sheer joy of a desert dweller for whom water has always represented the rarest of blessings.

Another wave burst over the side, and some of the rowers were swept off their benches. It made no difference; others took their places immediately, and continued to heave rhythmically, their powerful bodies shiny with the spray. Others seized wooden vessels and began bailing out the water that now surged up and down the gangway. When the ship almost stood on end on its stern, the water flooded into the canvas tent; a moment later, the flaps parted, and the big spider looked out. The velvety fur was plastered flat with water, and it seemed to radiate misery and helplessness. The woman saw it, and immediately pushed it back into the tent, pulling the flaps closed. The spider in the prow was lying in the bottom of its basket, from which the water ran in streams, its legs tightly bunched beneath it; only a movement in the black eyes betrayed that it was alive.

Looking over the side to see how the other ships were faring, Niall saw the big wave coming and braced himself to meet it, ducking his head. For a moment, the ship seemed to be full of water, and about to turn over. Then, miraculously, it righted itself. Niall felt something touching his icy flesh; looking down, he saw the forelegs of the spider locked round his waist; it had been washed out onto the deck. He could sense that it was mindless with fear, and would strike at him with his fangs if he tried to make it release its grip. So he stood there, clinging to the side, while the water flooded around his waist. Suddenly, the spider released its grip and was swept down the gangway as the ship plunged into another deep trough in the waves.

Niall's instinct was to respond to its misery and despair. He was feeling curiously unconcerned about the water that surged around him and threatened to knock him down. He had seen the ship survive one tremendous wave, and realised that it was buoyant as a cork. Even if filled with water, it would still not sink. And the wide, flat bottom and the deep keel; meant that it would be almost impossible to turn over. All Niall had to do was to make sure that he was not swept overboard. And when a coil of rope almost knocked his feet from under him, he seized the opportunity to tie one end round his waist and the other to the wooden capstan that held the anchor rope.

When the spider was washed back towards him, and seemed in danger of being swept over the side, Niall grabbed it by its forelegs and pulled it against him. It recognised this as a gesture of assistance and tried to wind its other legs around him. Since the spider was bigger than he was, this was impossible, and the next plunge of the boat almost wrenched it away again. The problem seemed to be that its body was more buoyant than Niall's, so each surge of water threatened to throw it the length of the ship. And, unlike human hands, the claws at the end of its legs were pathetically inadequate for taking a grip on the sides of the boat.

It was obvious to Niall that it needed something it could cling to. The safest place, quite obviously, was the basket, which was firmly attached to its place inside the great curving hollow of the prow. When the ship rode up a wave, this hollow filled with water; but at least it offered a kind of security. Niall staggered forward, hampered by the spider—whose fangs were still extended in instinctive response to terror—and steadied himself against the curving upright of the prow, which reared above him like a striking snake. For a few moments, the ship was level as it reached the bottom of a wave. Deliberately using his mind, Niall tried to make the spider understand that it should return to its place in the prow, and cling to the woven sides of the basket, whose lattice-like projections offered a grip for its claws. As another wave almost forced him to release his grip, the spider seemed to grasp what he was trying to convey; it released his body and, like some huge cat, heaved itself back into its basket. A moment later, another wave almost threw Niall on top of it; the prow filled with water; but when it subsided a moment later, the spider was still clinging to the sides of the basket.

Someone tapped him on the shoulder; it was the commander. She offered Niall a wooden bucket, and in sign language told him to start bailing. Niall tried to obey, but found it difficult; since he was at least a foot shorter than most of the sailors, he had to raise the full bucket above his head, and most of the water blew back on him. He sat down and clung to the bench.

There was a ripping sound, and Niall suddenly found himself engulfed in wet canvas; the wind had snapped two of the ropes holding the tent, tearing it from top to bottom. Now it was flapping like some huge sail. The spider inside it was hurled like a stone from a sling against one of the oarsmen, and knocked him backwards off his bench; then Niall found himself sharing his own bench with the struggling spider. He tried to extricate himself; as he did so, the ship lurched on to its side. The canvas struck him a violent blow on the shoulder. With a strange sense of slow motion, Niall found himself being carried over the side.

It all happened so quickly that there was no time for alarm. The wave carried him backwards, plunged him down to a depth of six feet, then brought him, blinded and gasping, back to the surface. As his gaze cleared, he saw the ship righting itself. The rope jerked at his waist, almost lifting him out of the water. In the momentarily calm sea, he grabbed it with both hands and tried to heave himself towards the ship. At that moment, he felt an arm groping at his back, trying to pull him down, and for an instant experienced total, blind panic. A hairy foreleg tried to wrap itself round his neck. Automatically, he lashed out with his feet, trying to kick himself free. The sea did the rest; the spider's grip was broken and it was swept away from him.

As this happened, Niall found himself staring for a moment into the expressionless black eyes, and he experienced its sense of despair and hopelessness as clearly as if it had called out to him. Quite suddenly, his own fear vanished. The spider was asking for aid, fully aware that Niall held the key to its life or death. Niall's instinctive response was to release his grip on the rope and launched himself towards the spider. Immediately, it ceased to struggle. Niall reached it a moment later and had to fight panic as the legs wound themselves round him. Then he remembered the rope. He grabbed it with both hands and tried to heave himself back towards the boat. A wave submerged him, but he continued to cling to the rope. Then he bumped against the boat's wooden side; arms were reaching down for him. The spider was still clinging tightly as they were both hauled out of the water. Hands grasped him under the shoulders and dragged him over the side. The sailors who were lifting him fell backwards, and Niall fell on top of them, the spider's legs still wrapped around them. He felt one of them snap as they struck the bench.

His lungs seemed to be full of water; he knelt there, his head on the bench, coughing and vomiting. Yet in spite of the lurching of the ship, which made the water surge around his waist, he felt a deep sense of relief and security to be able to cling once more to a solid object.

He was still clinging to the bench half an hour later, when the storm subsided. It seemed to happen quite suddenly; one moment he was being heaved up and down; the next, everything was still. He looked up and saw a patch of blue sky overhead. The wind became a mere breeze, and the water in the bottom of the ship ceased to surge back and forth and was suddenly as still as a pond. Sunlight warmed his bare back, and he felt he had never experienced such a wholly delightful sensation.

The ship was in chaos. Everything seemed to be afloat; ropes, barrels, sea chests, oars. Niall stood up and peered over the side; neither of the other two boats was visible. He waded to the other side and looked over; the sea was empty. But on the northern horizon he caught his first glimpse of land.

The sail was raised, and the tiller tied in position. Then everyone aboard helped to bail the ship. Within half an hour, there was only a narrow strip of water down the central aisle. Niall himself lent a hand, using a wooden ladle, and as he did so, experienced a glowing sensation of happiness to be working alongside the brawny sailors, playing his own small part in clearing up the chaos left behind by the storm. Now the danger was past, everyone was smiling and relaxed, and he was pleased to observe that they no longer ignored him but treated him as one of themselves.

One of the sailors handed him his pack. All the food in it, with the exception of the prickly pears, was ruined. But the heavy metal tube was still there; its weight had prevented the pack from being swept away.

The storm now seemed like a dream. The sun was beating down from an electric blue sky, and soon no trace of dampness remained on the boards. The two spiders were lying there absorbing the heat, one at either end of the ship. The spider Niall had rescued had lost its front claw as they struck the bench, and a trickle of blood ran from the broken leg. Niall observed that the sailors took care not to approach too close; not, obviously, out of fear, but out of respect and solicitude. They seemed to have an almost religious veneration for the spiders.

He was standing on a bench, straining his eyes towards

the approaching land, when someone tapped him on the shoulder. It was the commander, and she was holding a metal goblet in both hands. As she held it out towards him he saw that it contained a golden liquid that sparkled in the sun. He accepted with a smile of gratitude—the sea water had given him a raging thirst—and raised it to his lips with both hands. It was a sweet, fermented liquor, not unlike the drink brewed by his father, but richer and far more pleasant. The woman took the cup from him, looking into his eyes, and drank from the other side of the rim. Niall suddenly noticed that the sailors had ceased their work, and were all looking at him. He realised that the drink was not simply a friendly gesture, but some kind of ceremony. But what was its meaning? Then, as he looked past her to the big spider, which lay sprawled in the sun, one of its legs bent at an unnatural angle, he guessed the answer. It was a gesture of thanks for saving its life.

When she had drained the goblet, the commander smiled at him, then turned it upside down and allowed its last drop to fall onto the boards. She turned away, and the sailors resumed their work.

The drink induced a pleasant light-headedness, and a sensation of warmth in his veins. His weariness vanished. At the same time, he realised that his mind was in tune with the minds of the sailors; he could feel their joy that the storm was over, and that the ship was approaching land. But what surprised him was that he was still unable to perceive their thoughts as individuals. When he tried to look into the mind of any one of the sailors, it was as if he was looking *through* it, into someone else's mind, and then through that, and into someone else's, in a kind of infinite regress. It reminded him of looking into the minds of the ants. They seemed to share one another's identity.

The only exception to this was the commander. She

seemed to have her own confidence and individuality, the recognition that she had to make decisions and take on responsibilities. Yet even here, there was not the kind of individuality he had become accustomed to in his mother and Ingeld, and nothing remotely like the self-assurance of Merlew. It was as if a part of her mind were transparent, like clear water, totally unclouded by reflection or self-awareness.

One of the sailors gave a shout and pointed over the starboard side. Niall jumped to his feet and stared out across the smooth sea. In the blue haze of the distance, he could see the other two boats. It was all that was needed to complete his sense of happiness.

THE SHORE was now close, and Niall could make out a rocky coastline, with undulating cliffs, needles and pinnacles of seaworn granite and green fields sloping to the sea. The wind was a gentle breeze that carried them smoothly towards the land, as if to make up for its previous violence. As they came closer, he could see trees and yellow gorse, and a large bee zoomed past his ear. But there was no sign of people, or of human habitation.

The oarsmen began to row as the commander beat time. The ship followed the coastline in a westerly direction for perhaps two miles. Then, as they rounded a peninsula, Niall saw the first evidence of human handiwork—a harbour of white stone that reflected back the sun. Now the breeze dropped, and the heat increased. They passed a rocky islet on which were the remains of a tower; but most of its carved granite blocks lay around its base.

The harbour itself was the most impressive sight he had seen since the castle on the plateau: the great curving wall, twenty feet thick, built out into the sea, the massive dressed stones of the jetty, the strange wooden machine that towered into the air on the end of the quay, the fleet of boats moored inside the harbour; once again, Niall experienced a peculiar excitement at the thought that men like himself had once built this immense structure. Only at close quarters was it apparent that all this had been built a long time ago, and had been allowed to fall into semi-ruin.

Once inside the harbour bar, the rowers ceased to pull, and the boat glided across the still water under its own momentum. From the quay, a man threw down two of the thickest ropes Niall had ever seen, and these were secured to the prow and the stern. A gangplank was lowered. The commander was the first to cross. Then she knelt, her head bowed, as the two spiders followed her. Workers on the quay assumed the same attitude of homage, and remained in this position until the spiders had passed.

A sailor touched Niall on the elbow and indicated that he was to go next. He assumed he was to be escorted ashore as a prisoner, and was surprised to realise that he was expected to go alone, and embarrassed that the sailors stood to attention as he passed. The commander put out a hand to steady him as he stepped off the gangplank.

"What is your name?" It was the first time she had spoken to him.

"Niall. "

"A name of good fortune."

Niall failed to understand her. "Why?"

"You have earned the favour of the spiders. There can be no greater good fortune."

She took his arm and led him along the quay. The dock workers continued to stand to attention as they passed. They were, he observed, even bigger and more powerful than the sailors; he had never seen such muscles.

He asked diffidently: "Where are we going?" She looked so stern and purposeful that he half-expected her to ignore him. But she seemed to accept his right to question her.

"To the harbour master's."

She indicated the square, grey stone building at the end of the quay. Like the quay itself, this was in a poor state of repair, and its windows had been bricked up. The commander knocked on the door. In a moment, it was opened by one of the wolf spiders, which stood aside for them to enter. After the glare of the sunlight, it took Niall's eyes a few minutes to adjust to the darkness. He seemed to be in a large, empty room that smelt of damp and decay. Only a little light was admitted through cracks in the roof. He almost stumbled into the big wolf spider.

A cobweb sloped down from the rear corners of the room to within a few feet of where they were standing. In the centre of this web, looking directly at them, was a black death spider. It was smaller than the wolf spiders, and its black, shiny body was more bulbous than theirs. The single row of black eyes extended round its head like a row of beads. These, and the folded poison fangs, gave the face the same frightening, inscrutable expression he had observed in the spider he had killed.

Niall experienced an uncontrollable rush of fear, which communicated itself instantly to the spider. He could feel its will probing his own—not in the clumsy, inexpert manner of the wolf spiders, but with a subtlety that betrayed a sharp intelligence. What terrified him was the thought that the spider might be able to read his mind, and discover that he had killed a death spider.

His instinctive response to the probing was to become passive, and to blank his mind. The death spider was attempting to enter his brain, exactly as Niall had entered the brain of the tent spider. Since there was no point in resistance, Niall's reaction was to duplicate the mental vibration of the tent spider. In effect, he became the tent spider as naturally as a chameleon changes colour.

He could sense that the death spider found this puzzling. It half-recognised the vibration, but found it strange and unfamiliar. Its brain transmitted a communication to the brain of the big wolf spider; it was a single impulse, like a signal, and therefore as easy to interpret as a facial expression. It was saying, in effect: "He seems to be an idiot."

The reply-signal was a dubious gesture of assent, as if it had said: "I'm afraid so."

If this exchange had taken place in words, Niall's feelings would have betrayed him. Both the wolf spiders knew the truth about him. In the crisis of the storm, his mind had communicated directly with theirs, and no dissimulation was possible. But in the swiftness of the exchange of mental impulses, he had no time for fear, or even for relief that the wolf spider had not betrayed him.

The death spider turned its attention to the commander. Its will issued a blunt command: "Take him away." A moment later, Niall was out in the dazzling sunlight, unable to believe that the danger was over.

She noticed that he looked shaken.

"Were you afraid?"

Niall nodded. "Yes."

A gleam of sympathy came into her eyes.

"You don't have to be. They treat their servants well."

Niall wanted to ask more questions, but she cut him short. "I have to report to my captain. You'd better go and wait for your family to arrive."

Niall wandered back to the end of the quay. The sailors had all disembarked, and the ship was empty. No one seemed to pay him any attention. He asked one of the dock workers when they expected the other two ships. The man shrugged and said: "Soon." And since neither was in sight, Niall walked back along the quay. The big wooden tower-like structure now seemed to be in operation, and he was curious to see what it was used for.

He found it in a kind of inner harbour. A ship was being unloaded there. It had a flat bottom and was broader than the ship on which Niall had sailed. It was obviously a cargo vessel, the deck divided into bays to prevent its load from moving around in heavy seas. These were full of sacks of coarse brown cloth. A wheel at the base of the wooden structure made it possible to manipulate it over the ship, and a square platform was then lowered down to the deck on ropes; when it had been loaded with sacks, it was raised again and swung back onto the quay, where the sacks were loaded into a cart. To Niall, it seemed a miracle of engineering, and he sat and watched its movements with fascination.

He was also intrigued by the man who was supervising the unloading. He was much smaller than the brawny dockers who surrounded him—scarcely taller than Niall. He wore a shabby yellow tunic and a hat of peculiar design, with a peak that protected his eyes from the sun. He gave orders in a rapid, sharp voice, but with a strange accent that Niall found incomprehensible.

The man was obviously not a docker; neither did he seem to be one of the sailors. Idly, Niall tuned in to the little man's mind, and knew immediately that his speculation had been correct. This man's thought-vibrations were active and chaotic, quite unlike the disturbing, ant-like passivity of the sailors and dockers.

As he tried probing further, the man looked around uncomfortably, aware of this attempt to invade the privacy of his head—as Niall's own family would have been. A moment later, he glanced up at Niall. For a moment, Niall thought he was about to speak; then a sailor carrying a sack blundered against him, and the little man exploded with impatience. "Look where you're going, you flea-brained oaf!"

But ten minutes later, when the last of the sacks was unloaded, he climbed up the ladder and walked straight up to Niall. Niall, who was sitting on a capstan, looked up at him guilelessly. The man had a sharp, thin face with a large beak of a nose, and an almost bald head. He placed one hand on Niall's shoulder, peered into his face with mock aggression, and said:

"What the 'ell do you think you're playing at?"

Niall said: "I'm afraid I don't understand."

"You understand all right." He sat down on a sack, then said in a friendlier tone: "Where you from?"

Niall pointed. "The great desert."

The little man said: "Oh, you're one o' them, are you?"

Niall asked: "What are you called?"

"Bill."

"That is a strange name."

"No it's not. Where I come from it's a perfectly normal name. What's yours?"

"Niall."

"That's not a name, that's a river!"

Niall found his conversation as baffling as his accent. From his smile, it was apparent he was joking, but the joke was incomprehensible.

The little man looked at him from under lowered brows, as if trying to make a decision. He stared so long that Niall began to feel uncomfortable. Then the man said: "Who taught you to read minds?"

Niall answered readily: "Nobody taught me."

"Oh, come on!"

Niall found this puzzling. Come on where?

The little man decided to try a new line of questioning. "When did you arrive?"

"Half an hour ago. I'm still waiting for my mother and brother. They are out there." He pointed to the sea. As he did so, he saw that both ships were now in sight, about a mile offshore.

Again the little man stared into his eyes for an uncomfortable length of time. Niall was now anxious to get away to meet the ships. He stirred impatiently.

"Do it again," the man said.

"Do what?"

"What you did before."

It seemed easiest to comply, so Niall stared into the man's eyes, tuned in to his thought waves, then deliberately used his own mind as a probe.

The little man looked startled. He shook his head and said quietly: "Well, well, well."

Niall understood that. "Well what?"

"I don't know what the crawlies'll do when they find out."

"Crawlies?"

"The black bastards. The spiders. Creepy crawlies."

"What do you think they'll do?"

The little man placed the ball of his thumb on the palm of his other hand, and gave a violent twist. The meaning was perfectly clear. Niall felt his face grow pale. Now he no longer felt anxious to hurry away.

"Do you think they'll find out?" he asked.

The man shrugged. "I dunno. I've never worked out just what they *can* do and what they can't." He chewed his lip thoughtfully. "But I've got a feeling they don't know half as much as they'd like us to think."

Niall glanced out to sea. The ships appeared no closer. "Are you a servant of the spiders?"

The man shook his head violently. "No, thank God. I can't stand 'em. They give me the creeps."

"Then what do you do?"

"I work for the bombardiers."

"The beetles?"

"That's right."

"What kind of work?"

The man grinned. "Make bangs. I'm their chief explosives expert." He pointed to the sacks. "That stuff in there's for making gunpowder."

They were interrupted by one of the dockers. He stood to attention, saluted the little man, and said that the cart was ready to leave.

"All right. I'll be with you in a minute. Get ready to start." Waving him away, he waited until the docker was out of hearing, then leaned forward and said in a low voice: "Take my advice. Don't let the crawlies find out."

"All right." Niall tried to look more courageous than he felt.

The little man climbed on top of the sacks. The cart, which had two enormous wheels shod with iron, also had two shafts, each about ten feet long. Four muscular dockers seized each one of these and, at an order from the little man, began to heave. By the time they reached the end of the quay, they were moving at a steady trot. The little man turned and gave a brief wave. Niall waved back, and watched until the cart was out of sight. Then he walked thoughtfully back towards the main dock.

On the way there, he met the commander. She smiled at him—she seemed in a good mood—and gave him a thump with her clenched fist. He was aware that this was a friendly gesture, but he felt it had almost broken his shoulder.

"You need fattening up," she said.

"Fattening?" There was something about the way she said it that made him feel uneasy.

"The masters like us to be strong and healthy. Like that." She pointed to a passing docker whose muscles stood out on his arms like cables.

Niall said without conviction: "Yes, I'd like that."

Staring at her face, trying to read her expression, he found that he had automatically tuned in to her mind. He experienced nervous embarrassment, as if he had inadvertently bumped against her, and instantly withdrew his scrutiny. A moment later, it struck him that she seemed unaware of this contact of minds. Cautiously, prepared for instant withdrawal, he tried again. He at once became aware of why she was so pleased with herself—and with him. Her commanding officer had just congratulated her on bringing the wolf spiders safely back to land. If the spiders had been harmed, she would have been blamed and punished. And although it would not have been her fault, she would have accepted the blame and the punishment. As it was, she had received only praise, and consequently felt well disposed towards Niall.

All this Niall saw instantaneously, simply by tuning in to her feeling-waves. Once he had assured himself that she was unaware of his scrutiny, he continued to probe her mind. It was an odd sensation. By tuning in to her consciousness, Niall felt as if he was inside her head, looking out through her eyes. He was aware of her female body, of the bronzed breasts that bounced as she walked, and the long legs whose stride forced him to hurry to keep up. For the moment, he had ceased to be Niall and become this tall, beautiful woman. He was even aware of her name: Odina.

But why was she unaware that he was inside her head?

The answer, he realised, had something to do with that strange blankness that he sensed inside the minds of these people. It was as if a part of their consciousness was anaesthetised.

Then, suddenly, he began to see an outline of the answer. It had to do with the spiders. These people were so accustomed to their minds being probed by the spiders that they took it for granted. Their minds had open doors, so anyone could wander in and out . . . like the pepsis wasp, that was so used to being handled it made no attempt to sting, even when one of the children tried to stroke it.

They had reached the end of the quay. The nearest ship was just passing the outer harbour wall. Niall felt a thrill of delight as he recognised Veig's face looking over the side, and he waved vigorously. Veig waved back. As the ship was hauled against the quay, Niall could see that its port side had been damaged, its upper planks smashed as if by a heavy downward blow.

Five minutes later, the commander came ashore, followed by the wolf spider escort. Behind them came Veig. Niall started to run towards his brother, but was stopped by something that seemed to knock the breath from his body. The wolf spider was glaring balefully at him, and the beam of its will had stopped him like a heavy blow. Then, having made its point, the spider marched on past the kneeling commanders. It was evidently in a thoroughly bad temper.

Odina touched Niall on the shoulder, and raised her finger reproachfully.

"When the masters walk by, the slaves lower their eyes."

Niall said meekly, "I'm sorry."

He and Veig were made to stand to one side as the sailors disembarked. Niall whispered: "Where have you been? What happened?"

"The mast blew down in the storm—almost capsized us. Luckily, the other boat stayed with us . . ."

The commander of his ship gave him an angry glare. "Talking among prisoners forbidden."

Veig said: "Sorry."

They stood there silently, watching the other ship approach. Out of the corner of his eye, Niall observed them as they talked. Evidently Odina was telling her colleague what had happened in the storm. The woman stared at Niall with astonishment and disbelief. Then she strode over to them, looked into their faces for a moment, and said: "All right talking permitted." She turned her back and walked off.

Veig said: "What on earth was all that about?"

Niall whispered: "I'll tell you later."

The other ship had been moored farther along the quay. This time, Niall and Veig kept silent, their eyes averted, as the commander came ashore followed by a wolf spider. Behind them came Siris. They waited until the spider was twenty yards away before they rushed to embrace her. She was looking pale and ill. As Veig was hugging her, Niall caught the thought of one of the dockers; he was thinking: "What a skinny woman—*I* wouldn't like to kiss her . . ." Niall experienced a flash of protective indignation as he looked at his mother; to him, she seemed slim and beautiful. These slaves of the spiders had a strange idea of beauty . . .

Odina touched Niall's arm. "Come."

As they followed her along the quay, they heard one of the commanders ask, with no attempt to lower her voice: "Why are they coming with us?"

"The master's orders," Odina said.

Beyond the quays, they crossed a wide area of waste ground, covered with damaged boats, broken carts and piles of litter. The walls that surrounded the docks had been allowed to fall into a state of ruin. Evidently this had once been a large and flourishing port; now it had shrunk to a small harbour. Only the road underfoot seemed in a good state of repair; it was made of some hard, smooth substance like a continuous sheet of marble.

Beyond the dock wall, they came upon a row of hand carts, similar in design to the one Niall had already seen, but smaller. A dozen or so bored looking men were standing around. When Odina snapped her fingers, six came running and bowed in front of her. Odina and the two commanders climbed into one of the carts; two men seized each of its shafts, and stood waiting for further orders. Odina pointed to another cart, and then signalled Niall, Veig and Siris to climb in. As they did so, one of the men who took the shafts exclaimed: "Niall!"

"Massig!" Niall recognised him immediately as one of the group that had come to escort him to Kazak's underground city.

They locked forearms, but as they did so, one of the commanders snapped: "That's enough!" Massig went pale and hastily stood to attention. Odina gave an order. Her own four men went off at a sharp trot; the other cart followed them. Niall looked with concern and astonishment at the back of Massig's head. The hair, which had once been so beautifully washed and groomed, was now tangled and dirty.

The landscape around them was flat and desolate. There were ruined houses on both sides of the road, most of them only a few feet high. Ahead the road ran straight as an arrow to the top of a range of low hills. Outside the ruined town, the scenery improved, with green fields and trees, but remained oddly depressing. With its tangle of weeds and undergrowth, with the occasional ruined wall or barn, it looked as if it had survived some terrible disaster.

The runners proceeded at a steady jog-trot so long as the road was level; but when it began to slope gently upwards towards the hills, their pace slowed. Niall could tell from Massig's movements that he was tiring, and the thought distressed him; yet there was obviously nothing he could do about it. Finally, when the slope became so steep that the men had to slow to a walk, he leaned forward and tapped the nearest man on the shoulder.

"Would you like us to get out and walk?"

The man was so astonished that he stopped, and the others had to stop too.

"Walk?" The man shook his head in bewilderment. "Why?"

"So as not to tire you."

He shook his head. "Oh no. We'd get into terrible trouble if you did that."

"Why?"

"Because it's our job to pull you. If we didn't, the masters'd want to know why." He turned his back again, and began to heave. Massig shot Niall a sympathetic glance, as if to say: Thanks for trying anyway.

Half an hour later, the cart reached the top of the hill. Below them, enclosed in the hollow bowl of the hills, lay the spider city he had seen in his vision by the well. It was a city of tall square towers—towers that, in reality, were even greater than in his vision. And even at this distance, he could see the enormous cobwebs that stretched between them. Most of the towers were grey; a few were almost black. May were obviously little more than ruins, yet even the ruins were taller than the great columns of twisted rock near their home in the desert. Niall had never seen anything so breathtaking; it was like a city built by giants.

And in the centre of this grimy city, standing alone in its own green space, stood the white tower. It was not as tall as many of the surrounding buildings, but it stood out from them in its pure, blinding whiteness. In the sunlight, it sparkled as if lit from within by its own dazzling sun. Unlike the other towers, this tower was cylindrical, although the top was slightly narrower than its base. It might have been a slender white finger, pointing at the sky.

Niall looked at the faces of his mother and brother, and saw their feelings were the same as his own. It was a strange moment. For many days now, they had known that this was their destination. Yet the city of the spiders had remained a dream. They were not even afraid of it, because it seemed an unreality. Now suddenly it was real, and the sensation was like waking from a dream. It was far more real and frightening than Niall had imagined; its stained towers somehow resembled ruined teeth in the face of a skull. Even without the giant cobwebs it would have been ugly and menacing. Yet the white tower, in its square green space, seemed indifferent to the ugliness and menace. It aroused in Niall a curious spark of pure joy, and he sensed that Veig and Siris also felt this. It seemed oddly familiar, as if he had often seen it in dreams.

The runners, who had paused to regain their breath, now began the descent to the city. Although steeper than the uphill route, this was less difficult, for the cart had brakes that the runners operated from the shafts, so they could check its forward rush. Relieved of his anxiety about Massig—who was now walking at a comfortable pace—Niall was able to relax and pay more attention to his surroundings. What surprised him here was the beauty of the scenery. It had evidently been raining—black clouds still hung over the distant hills—and the grass and bushes glistened with it. Halfway down the slope, the road plunged into woodland, and the sun vanished. These were not the bare, hardy trees of the desert; some of them had trunks five feet in diameter, while their branches over-arched the road and formed a green tunnel; others stretched up so high that he could not see the sky through the maze of branches. The grass between the trees was so green that it looked like the weed in the bottom of a slow-flowing stream. When they passed between two high banks, Niall was able to pluck a few blades and chew them; they were sweet and succulent, and their taste seemed to bring a vision of endless forests.

Then, suddenly, they were out of the woods, their eyes dazzled again by the evening sunlight, and the black and grey city was directly ahead. The contrast was strange and somehow unbelievable, as if either the woods or the city must be and illusion. The fields on either side of the road were now cultivated, and they could see a few men working in them. Then the road—which remained as smooth as marble—ran along by the side of a river whose waters looked deep and black. Half a mile later, they were crossing a bridge, its iron towers half rusted away. Underneath the bridge was a 50-foot cobweb; lurking in its corner, in the darkness of rust-stained masonry, he caught a glimpse of black eyes peering out at them.

Then they were in the spider city, and the great towers formed solid ranks on either side. They were so tall that Niall had to tilt back his head to see the strip of blue evening sky above. Many were ruined; he could see through their empty windows into bare rooms with collapsing walls. At street level, steps often descended down behind rusting iron railings to invisible rooms below, and men and women seemed to use these constantly. The sheer number of people t.ok his breath away; they seemed to be hurrying in all directions like the ants beyond the rocky wilderness. The majority were men—all tall, powerful and muscular—but there were also a number of women and girls. Most of these wore tunics that covered their breasts but left their arms bare; a few, he noticed, wore dresses that also covered their arms. One tall, bare breasted woman who crossed the road in front of them was so like Odina that Niall had to peer into the distance to make sure the three commanders were still in their vehicle, which was now about a quarter of a mile ahead of theirs.

Evening was drawing on, and the towering buildings excluded the sunlight. As the streets grew darker, the people disappeared. When their cart finally came to a halt, the streets were almost deserted. Their runners placed the shafts on the ground and helped them to descend. Odina came out of the darkness, placed her hand on Niall's shoulder and pointed.

"They will show you where you are to sleep. You are to live with the charioteers."

Niall said: "Thank you," because he could think of nothing else to say.

"Don't thank me. Thank Krol."

"But who is Krol."

"The master you saved."

"The spider who . . ."

"Ssshh!" She placed her hand fiercely over his mouth and glanced up into the air. "Never use that word! Here they are the masters. If one of them approaches, bow down before him. Otherwise you'll soon find yourself in the great happy land."

"Great happy land?"

"Don't ask so many questions. Curiosity killed the bat." She turned to one of the runners. "What is you name?"

"Daraul."

"Daraul, I give them into your charge. Your life for theirs." The man made a gesture of homage. "You will receive your orders in the morning." She seized Niall's ear and gave it a friendly twist that made his eyes water. "Sleep well, little savage."

"Thank you."

She strode off into the darkness.

The man called Daraul was the one to whom Niall had made the suggestion about walking. Now he had seen Niall treated with some degree of familiarity by the commander, his attitude became more friendly. "Follow me, all of you. Be careful of the steps—they're broken."

Massig took Niall's arm. "I'll help you."

They descended the steps into the dark basement area. Someone pushed open a creaking door. The smell of burning oil met them, and they entered a large, dimly lit room. It seemed to be full of men, many of them lying or sitting on low bunks or beds. When Siris came into the room, some of them stood to attention, and one started to sink onto one knee.

"There's no need for that," Daraul said. "These are only savages from the desert." He said it without contempt, merely stating a fact.

One of the men said: "Then what are they doing here?"

"I don't know. It's orders from above."

As if relieved of some burden on their attention, the men turned away and ignored the newcomers. Some were eating food from bowls, others were sewing or repairing sandals. The room was warm from the heat of their bodies and smelt of sweat.

Massig touched Daraul's arm. "If you like, I'll look after them and find them somewhere to sleep."

Daraul looked at him with the same blank incomprehension that he had shown when Niall offered to get out of the cart. Massig put his hand on Niall's shoulder. "He's a friend of mine. We'd like to talk."

"What about?" Daraul asked.

"Oh, all kinds of things—how we got here, for example."

Daraul shrugged, still looking baffled. "Oh, all right."

It struck Niall that Daraul, like most of the other men in the room, was of a low degree of intelligence, but in no way hostile.

During the next half hour, Massig found beds for them. They had to carry oil lamps and walk along a black corridor to some remote part of the basement. In a big, musty-smelling room there were dozens of beds in various states of disrepair. Fortunately, their legs seemed interchangeable, fixing into wooden sockets, so they were able to assemble three relatively undamaged frames. These they carried back to the main room, Massig helping Siris with hers. Another dusty room revealed piles of ancient mattresses stuffed with fragments of rag, while another was filled with blankets, many rotting with damp. Niall was too tired to care. Siris yawned so much that they left her lying on Massig's bed while they went in search of pillows—these were made of wood and covered with a thin layer of leather; when they returned, she was fast asleep.

Next Massig took them to the communal kitchen; this was uncomfortably hot, due to a huge iron stove which had been stoked with firewood. There seemed to be an abundance of vegetables, and even a big metal bowl filled to the top with some dubious-looking meat. Niall was too tired to cook; he settled for a bowl of a green coloured soup from a tureen on the stove, with a chunk of hard brown bread. This tasted far better than it looked—in fact, was so full of interesting flavours that he went back for a second helping. Their beds were erected in a corner of the basement room, and they sat and ate with their backs propped against the wall. The man in the next bed to Niall looked at him in a friendly way and said: "You're too thin. We'll soon fatten you up." It was a remark he was to hear constantly during the course of the next day or so. It was not simply a jocular comment, intended to make conversation, but a serious observation, stated with deep conviction. Among the charioteers, eating seemed almost a religion.

While they ate, Niall listened to the conversation that went on around them. He was hoping to achieve some insight into the minds of the human inhabitants of the spider city. But he soon grew bored. The men seemed obsessed by various games—many of them played a game that involved a handful of carved wooden sticks—and talked endlessly about a long-awaited match between the charioteers and the food gatherers in two days' time, involving some kind of ball. There were times when Niall had the hallucinatory feeling that he had accidentally tuned in to the collective mind of the ants. Yet for all their obvious lack of intelligence, these men seemed good natured and kindly enough, and once they had become accustomed to the presence of Niall and his companions, treated them as if they were all part of a large family group. After a lifetime of reliance on himself and his small family, Niall found this sense of communal identity rather pleasant and relaxing.

As they ate, Massig described how Kazak's city had been overrun. The story was soon told. Two days after Ulf and Niall had left for home, the antherds had failed to return in the evening. A search party, led by Hamna, had also failed to return. The next morning, when Massig woke up, he found himself unable to move . . . Niall could already guess the rest of the story. The spiders marched straight into the city, led by one of the antherds, who was terrified out of his wits. No one stood a chance. Many men were killed. In Massig's opinion, this was not because they showed signs of resistance, but simply because the spiders were hungry. A number of children were also killed and eaten. The rest had been taken away, and were now here in the spider city under the care of nurses.

There seemed to be hordes of spiders—hundreds of them, mostly the brown wolf spiders (whom Massig called soldiers). It was they who organised the long march to the sea. Massig admitted that this was less of an ordeal than he expected. They were well fed, and when anyone showed signs of exhaustion, the spiders either allowed them to rest or ordered them to be carried on improvised stretchers. When the prisoners arrived in the spider city, all were in relatively good health.

Massig described how they were paraded in the main square, in front of the white tower, and the mothers reunited with their children. But this was not to last. The men were divided into groups and assigned to various tasks. Some became food gatherers, some agricultural workers, some city workers, some—like Massig—charioteers. The women were not separated; they were taken, all together, to the central part of the city reserved for women. For, Massig explained, women were revered in the city of the spiders. Among spiders, the female is more important than the male—she often eats him after courtship. The spiders found the human system of treating women as household slaves deeply offensive to their natural instincts. So women were trained to be the masters, men the servants. Since the women of Kazak's city had become accustomed to domination by the males, they would have to be re-educated. Until they learnt to assume their new role as masters, they would be kept segregated from their husbands.

Niall asked: "And what about the children?" He was thinking of his sisters.

"They're kept in a nursery not far from the women. But the women won't be allowed to see them until they've been re-educated."

Massig had now been here about a month. The work was hard but he had no serious complaints. Every morning the charioteers had to report to the square at the centre of the Women's Section; their job was to take the overseers to work—some to the fields, some to the docks, some to other parts of the city. It was not a bad job, especially if you could get the city run. The dock run was the hardest, and Massig suspected he had been assigned to it as a punishment; one of the women had overheard him referring to—here Massig looked nervously around and lowered his voice—referring to the masters as "spiders."

Niall was puzzled. "But what's wrong with that?"

"They say its disrespectful—talking about them as if they're insects."

"But I met a man in the docks who called them crawlies," Niall said.

"Sshh!" Massig looked round in alarm, but no one was listening. "Who on earth was that?"

"A man with a funny name—Bill, I think he said . . ."

"Oh, he's not one of us. He works for the beetles. His name's Bill Doggins." He said it with contempt, and Niall was secretly amused at the way Massig had already learned to identify with his fellow workers.

"Billdoggins?"

"Bill Doggins. He's got two names for some reason. The men who work for the beetles says it's an old tradition."

Veig leaned forward and asked in a low voice: "Do you think there's any chance of escaping from here?"

Massig looked horrified. "No! Not the slightest. Where would you escape *to*? They'd simply hunt you down. But why should you want to escape? It's not a bad life here."

"Well to begin with, I don't want to be a slave."

"Slave? But *we're* not slaves."

Veig asked ironically: "No? What are you?"

"We're servants. That's quite different. The real slaves live on the other side of the river. They're all idiots."

"Why, what's wrong with them?"

"I've told you—they're idiots, quite literally. They look like monsters." Massig did an imitation of a man with a slack jaw, glazed eyes and blubber lips.

"Why do they want slaves if they've got servants?" Niall asked.

"Oh, for the really nasty jobs, like cleaning the sewers. They also get eaten."

Niall and Veig said together: "Eaten?" They said it so loud that Siris opened her eyes for a moment.

"Yes. The spiders breed them for food."

Niall was fascinated and horrified. "Do *they* know that?"

Massig shrugged. "I think so. They just take it for granted. They're about as intelligent as ants."

Niall glanced around at the men who surrounded them, but said nothing.

"What about the . . . servants. Do they ever get eaten?" Veig asked.

Massig shook his head emphatically. "Oh no. At least, only under very unusual circumstances."

"Such as?"

"Well, for example, no one is allowed out after dark. There's a general rule that the spiders can eat anyone they catch out at night." He added quickly: "But of course, it never happens because no one is stupid enough to go out at night."

"But why don't they want people to go out after dark?"

"I suppose they want to stop husbands sneaking off to see their wives, or mothers trying to see their children."

Veig said scornfully: "And you mean to say you *like* it here?"

Massig looked defensive. "Well, I didn't say I liked it,

but . . . well, I suppose it could be worse. At least we get plenty of sunlight. In Dira, we were lucky if we saw the outside world once a month. And the food here is quite good—they like to keep you well fed. And we're allowed to play games every Saturday afternoon. We can apply to change jobs once a year—I'm going to try to be a sailor next year. And of course, we retire at forty."

"Retire? What's that?"

"We don't have to work any more. Instead, we go to the great happy land."

"The what?"

Before Massig could reply, there was a strange booming sound from outside; it made Niall's hair prickle on his scalp. It was repeated several times—a sound like the moaning of some gigantic creature in pain.

"My God, what's that?" Veig exclaimed.

"That means it's time for lights out. We have to get to sleep fairly early because we have to be awake at dawn."

The men in the room began extinguishing their oil lamps and climbing into bed. Only one lamp was left burning. All conversation died away.

"What's the great happy land?" Niall whispered to Massig.

Massig whispered: "Ssshh! We're not allowed to talk after lights out."

"Why?"

"I'll explain in the morning. Good night."

He turned his back on Niall and pulled the coverlet round his shoulders. The room was now quiet except for the sound of heavy breathing. It was oddly comforting to be among so many human beings. Within a few minutes, Niall had fallen into a deep and peaceful sleep.

It seemed that he had hardly closed his eyes when he was awakened by the sound of movements around him. One by one, the lamps were lit. Veig, always an early riser, was already out of bed. Siris, her long hair tangled with sleep, sat up and yawned. A man passing by the end of her bed made her a low bow.

Massig opened his eyes, peered around sleepily and pulled the blanket over his face. A moment later, he began to snore softly.

Then, to Niall's surprise, all the men in the room dropped to one knee in an attitude of obeisance. It took several moments before he noticed that a woman was standing inside the door. She looked like Odina—but then, all the commanders seemed to look alike.

In a clear, precise voice, she said: "The strangers will report to the parade ground with everyone else." Then she turned and went out. The room returned to its normal activity. And Massig, who had been awakened by her voice, threw back the coverlet and scrambled out of bed. He was looking pale and shaken.

"Do you think she noticed me?" he asked Niall.

"No, I'm certain she didn't."

Massig breathed a sigh of relief. "They're pretty strict about sluggards."

"Sluggards?" Niall had never heard the word.

"People who can't get up in the morning." He groaned. "That's the one thing I don't like about this place—they make you get up so early. In Dira, we never slept for less than twelve hours. And after an all-night party, I once slept right round the clock and missed a day . . ."

Niall asked: "What do we do now?"

"We eat. We're due on parade in an hour."

He led them into the kitchen, where vessels of food steamed on the stove. The cooks had been working since an hour before dawn. Massig helped himself to a bowl of the green soup and a plate piled with vegetables and meat. Niall and Siris took smaller quantities. Next to the kitchen there was a large dining hall, with long wooden tables. Veig was already seated, a full plate in front of him. He waved his spoon at them.

"This meat is very good. What's it called?"

"Rabbit."

"What's that?"

"A kind of rat with long ears. But they breed quicker than rats."

After that, Massig settled down to the serious business of eating, and only grunted in reply to their questions.

Niall observed that there was very little conversation in the rest of the room—only the sound of spoons on wooden platters, and the champing of jaws.

Even Siris ate well. After her long night's sleep, her cheeks had regained their colour. It would have been impossible for her not to notice the admiring glances cast at her as men passed their table, and although she kept her eyes on her plate, Niall could tell that she enjoyed it. For the past twenty years, the only men Siris had seen had been members of her own family; it must have been a strange experience to feel herself admired by a roomful of muscular and handsome males.

After they had finished eating, Massig showed them the washing arrangements. A nearby room full of dozens of wooden buckets, each filled to the brim with water. They were instructed to take one of these into the next room, a large, bare chamber whose stone floor was covered with narrow channels. There Niall and Veig were invited to remove their travelstained clothes, and to pour the water over themselves. Siris was conducted to a smaller room nearby. Massig handed them lumps of a grey-coloured root, and showed them how to dip it in the water, then rub it on the skin. The result was a sappy-smelling froth which seemed to dissolve the dirt away. They were allowed to help themselves to as many buckets of water as they wanted. To desert dwellers, this seemed an unbelievable and delightful extravagance. So did the method of drying to which Massig introduced them—rubbing themselves all over with large rectangles of a rough and absorbent cloth.

When Siris emerged from her own private washroom with her skin glowing and her hair soaked with water, Niall thought he had never seen his mother looking so beautiful. He contemplated his own shining skin and clean hands and feet with a certain complacent satisfaction; he was beginning to understand why Massig liked this place.

Ten minutes later, they were assembled in the street outside. Now he could see it in broad daylight, Niall found it at once frightening and rather exciting. The tall grey buildings towered above them like cliffs, and cobwebs with strands like ropes stretched between them, some of them flat, some almost vertical. Many of the webs had obviously been there for years, for they were thick and furry with an accumulation of dust. A huge fly, its body as large as a man's head, smacked into one of these webs and sent down a shower of assorted debris, including wings of long-dead flies. The fly rebounded, soared upwards, and encountered another web, this one almost invisible, in which it buzzed frantically. Almost instantaneously, a black spider scurried across the web and leapt on the fly; a second later, the buzzing had ceased, and the fly hung limply as the spider swathed it in silk. Now Niall understood why the spiders left their old webs hanging there, instead of re-absorbing them into their bodies in the frugal manner of most spiders. Flying creatures took care to avoid the old webs, which were conspicuous, and blundered into the new ones, which were almost transparent.

At an order from Daraul, the men stood to attention; at

another barked command, they began to march down the centre of the street. At the next intersection, they turned right into a wider avenue. Niall experienced an upsurge of joy as he saw, in the distance, the white tower outlined against the blue morning sky.

They passed another platoon of men, travelling in the opposite direction. Niall could tell at a glance that these were the slaves of whom Massig had spoken. They wore drab grey smocks and were shambling rather than marching; their faces were blank, with drooling mouths and eyes that seemed incapable of focusing properly; their limbs often seemed to be crooked and distorted.

"Where are they going?" Niall whispered to Massig.

He shrugged. "To work. They're either the latrine squad or the sewer squad."

This wide avenue was in a better state of repair than the narrower streets. Some of it buildings were breathtaking, stretching up to such heights that Niall had to bend his head right back to see the rooftops. Some of them had elaborate domes on top. One vast, square building seemed to be built of green marble and had columns like the ruined temple in the desert. Others had large ground-floor windows made of some clear, transparent substance that reflected the light. Another seemed to be built entirely of this transparent substance, and its strange, curving planes were full of distorted reflections of the surrounding buildings. Niall tried to imagine what the original inhabitants of this extraordinary city must have been like, but found the task beyond his narrow experience. He could only suppose that they must have been a race of giants, or very great magicians. But in that case, how did the spiders defeat them?

The avenue was longer than it looked. It was half an hour before they emerged into a great open space directly opposite the white tower. There was a wide plaza, paved with the smooth, marble-like substance, and on the far side of this the broad space of emerald-green grass that surrounded the white tower. Facing the tower, at the end of the avenue, there was an even taller building whose lower storeys were faced with black marble and whose upper part seemed in an excellent state of repair. This soared above all the other buildings in the plaza. And it differed from these buildings in another respect; it had no windows. Closer inspection revealed that its windows had all been sealed up with some white substance so that they showed up as faint squares against the surrounding grey. Facing the white tower across the great open space, it created the inescapable impression of presenting it with a deliberate challenge.

Daraul made them line up in two ranks, facing the black façade. Then he ordered Niall, Veig and Siris to stand to one side. A few minutes later, a woman came out of the building. For a moment, Niall thought it was Odina, then realised that this woman was taller. She was dressed in a uniform of a black, shiny substance that left her arms bare.

"Stand to attention," Daraul muttered. "Chins up."

The woman marched across to them and surveyed the men with a hard, piercing gaze. They stared in front of them as if made of wood. Halfway down the line, she paused before a man who stood half a head taller than the rest. He had immense biceps and a chin like a rock.

"Your eyes moved," she said.

Still staring straight in front of him, the man said: "I'm sorry, commander."

The woman raised her hand as if to slap his face; the man tensed to receive the blow. Then, suddenly, she seemed to change her mind. Her fist clenched and hit him with tremendous force in the solar plexus. The man gasped and doubled up. The woman stepped back, and kicked him in the face. He was so heavy that the blow failed to make him reel backwards; instead, he sank onto his knees; the woman drew back her boot and dealt him another kick under the chin. With a groan, the man collapsed, his arms outspread, and a trickle of blood ran onto the marble. None of the other men stirred an inch. The commander glanced quickly up and down the line to make sure that no one had moved, then marched on and finished her inspection. Finally, she turned to Daraul.

"Very well, you can assign their duties." She came and stood in front of Niall, Veig and Siris; all were attempting to maintain an unflinching stare. Niall observed that she had a faint, ironic smile.

"Which of you is Niall?"

Hardly daring to move his lips, Niall said: "I am."

"Oh." She looked surprised. She stood in front of Veig for a long time and felt his muscles, then gave him a gentle blow in the stomach with her fist. "You're stronger than you look."

Veig stared straight in front of him, unmoving.

She looked contemptuously at Siris, felt her arm, then ran her hand down over her body; Niall could sense that his mother was trying hard not to flinch.

"You look strong enough," the woman said, "but you need fattening up. And we'll have to do something about your breasts." She turned on her heel and snapped: "Follow me." She marched back towards the black-fronted building. Niall and Veig glanced at each other, then followed her. Behind them, Daraul began giving orders.

The double doors of the building were at least ten feet high and proportionately wide. Outside, in the shade of the portico, two big wolf spiders stood on guard. They were evidently of a lowly rank, for the woman ignored them. Niall, Veig and Siris followed her into a dimly lit hallway; it took time for their eyes to become accustomed to its gloom after the dazzling morning sunlight. To their right was a wide marble staircase; two more wolf spiders stood guard at its foot. Although his sun-dazzled eyes could scarcely see them in the semi-darkness, Niall was interested to observe that they seemed to regard him with curiosity; he could sense the impulse that passed between them.

They followed her to the next floor, where she paused to speak to a woman dressed in the same black uniform, and who might, in the dim light, have been her twin sister. Here Niall sensed powerful will-vibrations which seemed to be issuing from an open door. He peered in and saw a large hall full of wolf spiders. They were standing in orderly ranks, and on a raised platform, facing them, a large black death spider was shouting orders—or what, in human language, would have been orders. The telepathic will-vibrations were so strong that even Veig appeared to notice them. They were apparently beyond Siris's psychic range, although when a particularly furious shout echoed through the building, she gave a start of suprise.

The woman finished her conversation and beckoned them to follow her again. She led them up three more flights of stairs, each guarded by two wolf spiders. The third flight was covered with a heavy carpet which yielded softly under their feet. The two guards who stood at the top of this flight were black death spiders. The woman spoke to them.

"The prisoners are here to see the Death Lord."

Niall observed that she spoke in a loud, clear voice as if addressing someone slightly deaf. And the spiders, who could sense the vibrations of her voice without being able to hear it, responded directly to her meaning. One of them sent back a message that meant: "Pass." And the woman was sufficiently attuned to its thought vibration to understand the order. It was the first instance Niall had observed of direct communication between a human being and a spider.

She beckoned to them. Suddenly, for the first time since he had been in this city, Niall experienced a rush of panic. He was remembering Jomar's stories of Cheb of the Hundred Eyes, and the legend of the Great Betrayal, when Prince Hallat taught Cheb to understand the secrets of the human soul.

This sense of unease swept upon him so quickly that it was like a sudden storm. The more he tried to subdue it, the more the waves of panic battered against his defences. What if the Spider Lord realised that he was responsible for the death of the spider in the desert? For one insane moment, he contemplated confessing everything, and flinging himself on the Spider Lord's mercy. He experienced a momentary gleam of hope, then thought of the swollen body of his father and knew it was an illusion.

The black door that faced him was cushioned with the same shiny material as the woman's uniform, and studded with nails that gleamed yellow in the half-light. The two death spiders who stood guard there seemed to be awaiting an order. Niall stared at it, frozen with misery and terror. Then he noticed that their escort was also nervous, and for some reason this observation brought him a spark of comfort. It was partly malicious satisfaction that the bully who had kicked a man in the face should herself be subject to fear. But there was also some deeper cause for satisfaction that eluded him.

By some process of association, he found himself thinking of the castle on the plateau. This was the image that enabled him to begin to fight the panic. It was the thought that it had been built by men, and that men had once been the lords of the earth, that provided the rallying point for his scattered resources of courage. He concentrated hard; it was difficult to maintain in the face of the panic, but he persisted. Then, suddenly, the light seemed to glow inside his skull, a single pinpoint of control and optimism. In the state of calm that followed, he realised suddenly that they were not waiting to be taken into the presence of the Death Lord. They were already in his presence. It was the Death Lord who was sending out this vibration of panic that had almost destroyed his control.

The door swung open. Their escort prostrated herself on the floor. Then, at an order from the guard, she entered the room on her hands and knees. She was so nervous that she had forgotten to beckon them to follow. Siris reached out and took the hands of her two sons; it was she who took the first step across the threshold of the Death Lord.

With a shock, Niall realised that this dark hall was familiar. So were the invisible eyes that watched him from a tunnel of grey cobwebs. This was the place that he had seen as he stared into the well in the country of red sandstone.

The will of the invisible presence issued an order; the woman crawled to the side of the room and remained kneeling. From the shadows, the eyes contemplated the three prisoners and tried to read their minds. Nothing was visible among the cobwebs, not even a stir of movement. And Niall was also still, for he felt that the slightest movement, either of his body or his mind, would expose them all to danger.

It was a strange sensation: facing this maze of cobwebs, and recognising the presence of a personality that stared out at them from the darkness. As a child, Niall had often been aware when someone was looking at the back of his head. This was much the same feeling, but a hundred times as strong. Before this moment, King Kazak had been the strongest personality he had ever encountered. But Kazak seemed a child to the will that now probed his own.

Niall made no attempt to simulate the mind-vibrations of the tent spider; an instinct told him that it would be pointless. He was dealing with an intelligence that was, in most respects, far greater than his own, and that would see through the deception. Instead, he merely closed his mind, while appearing to remain open and passive.

A violent blow struck him in the chest and hurled him backwards. He landed on the wooden floor with a crash that drove all the breath out of his body. Siris, who had heard and felt nothing, looked round in astonishment, then ran to help him. Another invisible blow caught her across the shoulders and knocked her spinning, so she fell on one knee. Veig, bewildered and uncertain, stared at them and wondered what was happening; to him it looked as if his family had suddenly flung themselves into random motion.

A voice inside Niall's chest said clearly: "Get up." The instruction was so clear it was as if it had been whispered in his ear. Niall's impulse to obey was instantly checked by some deeper impulse that told him to ignore it. This impulse was like a counter-command, and it overruled his fear.

Again, the voice said: "Get up." Niall pushed himself into a sitting position, then staggered to his feet. His shoulder was bruised, and the back of his head throbbed from contact with the floor. Yet the physical pain had its advantages. It enabled him to avert his mind from the relentless will that tried to force him to reveal himself.

He felt the force close round his body like a gigantic fist, squeezing his breath away. It was trying to show him that it could, if it so desired, crush him into a pulp. Niall was aware that this was true; yet oddly enough, it failed to intimidate him. An intuitive logic told him that his invisible tormentor would not be trying to frighten him if it intended to destroy him.

To Veig and Siris, it looked as if Niall had floated clear of the ground and was hovering in the air. Then Veig saw the pain on his brother's face and rushed forward. His hands encountered Niall's shoulders, which were pinched and constricted, and tried to pull him down to earth again. The force struck Veig, and sent him hurtling across the room so that he crashed into the wall. Siris screamed and ran to help him; this time, she was allowed to reach him. At the same moment, Niall was suddenly released and fell to his knees.

Their guard had leapt to her feet as Veig struck the wall within a few feet of her. Now she screamed: "Stand to attention!" But Niall was aware that the order came, not from her, but from the watcher in the shadows.

They obeyed her automatically. All three stood there, staring into the darkness, waiting for what would happen next. Of the three, only Niall was aware that the Death Lord was wondering whether to kill them immediately. He was also aware of an incredible fact: that this powerful being who now faced them was self-divided and troubled. The nature of the conflict eluded him. He was only aware that the Death Lord wanted to kill them, and at the same time recognised that this would solve nothing.

He was not afraid that his life hung in the balance; there was no time to be afraid. Neither was he relieved when he realised, a moment later, that their lives were to be spared.

The voice in his chest said: "You can go." For a moment, Niall was almost tricked into moving. Again, a deeper impulse stopped him. It was as if a third person were present inside him. He stood there, waiting, as the minutes passed. The room was completely silent. There was not the slightest stir among the cobwebs.

He felt the command before it was transmitted by their

guard. She shouted: "All right, turn round!" And, when they obeyed her, "Follow me!" She opened the door, stood aside for them to pass, then made a low obeisance before closing it again. Niall was aware that the invisible watcher continued to observe him as they followed her down the stairs. It ceased only as he stepped out into the sunlight.

Veig and Siris looked badly shaken. Both had believed themselves on the point of death; even now, they were not sure the danger was over.

Their guard was aware that something strange had taken place, and that Niall was somehow responsible for this. She looked at him oddly, trying to understand why this slim, brown-skinned youth, with his blue eyes and clean-cut features, should be of interest to the Lord who controlled so many destinies.

Niall could have answered her question. He had known the answer ever since he heard the voice of the Spider Lord inside his chest and felt the immense power of his will crushing his body.

The two of them had met before. Their minds had confronted one another as Niall gazed into the cistern in the red desert. Ever since then, the Death Lord had been consumed with curiosity to know more of this human creature whose mind could leap across the barriers of space. He wanted to know whether Niall understood the nature of his own powers, and whether he knew how to control them.

And now, after seeing Niall, he knew as little as ever. The questions remained unanswered. But he was capable of waiting. The patience of a spider has no limits.

On the low wall that surrounded the building, a man was sitting with his head in his hands. As their guard approached, he jumped to his feet and stood to attention. Niall recognised him as the man she had kicked in the face. One of his cheeks was swollen grotesquely, and there was a cut across the bridge of his nose; one eye was turning black.

"Take these people to the supervisor," the woman said.

The man nodded smartly. She turned on her heel and went back into the building.

"Come on." The man led them across the square to a two-wheeled cart parked on the grass. He raised its shafts and indicated that they were to get in. Siris, looking sympathetically at his battered face, said: "We don't mind walking. Just tell us where to go."

The man shook his head, as Niall had known he would. "Sorry. Got to obey orders." Unwillingly, they climbed into the cart.

Now, for the first time, Niall noticed men at the base of the white tower, and that one of them was wearing a yellow tunic. He tapped the man on the shoulder.

"What are they doing?"

He glanced across the grass without interest. "They're beetlemen. We're not allowed to speak to them."

"Why not?"

"Don't know. We don't ask questions." He broke into a jog-trot, jerking them backwards in their seats. Niall looked back curiously towards the tower. The men were carrying barrels from four-wheeled carts and placing them at the base of the tower. The little man in the yellow tunic seemed to be giving the orders.

Their charioteer trotted briskly along the wide avenue, apparently without effort. Except for a few wolf spiders, and a platoon of slaves marching in the distance, it was almost deserted. Niall leaned forward and asked their charioteer:

"Where are all the people?"

The man said laconically: "Working."

Niall tuned in to the charioteer's mind, and observed with

surprise that he felt no resentment towards the woman who had kicked him. He felt that it was his own fault, and that he deserved his punishment. Niall found such an attitude incomprehensible.

In front of a green building with columns like the ruined temple the charioteer lowered the shafts to the ground and helped them out.

"This way."

He led them up a flight of badly worn steps to a pair of elaborately decorated bronze doors, one of which he pushed open. Inside, they found themselves in a large hall with a grey marble floor; around the wall at intervals were marble benches. Huge windows filled the place with sunlight.

A woman was walking up the wide staircase. The charioteer cleared his throat and said: "Pardon me . . ."

The woman turned round and said: "Good God, Siris! What on earth are you doing here?"

Siris recognised the voice; it took her a moment longer to associate it with the face. Then she cried: "Ingeld!" and ran to embrace her. For a few moments, both women laughed aloud, and Ingeld swung Siris clear of the ground. Then she noticed the charioteer, who was kneeling on one knee.

"Where are you taking them?" she asked.

"To the supervisor, m'lady."

"That's all right. I'll take them. You wait down here." She turned to Niall and Veig. "So they captured you too. I thought they would."

Siris asked: "Are you a prisoner?"

Ingeld smiled and raised her eyebrows.

"Not exactly . . ."

Veig was looking at her stomach. "I thought you were pregnant?"

Ingeld said casually: "Fortunately, it was a false alarm."

Niall and Veig exchanged glances. Niall knew what his

brother was thinking: that Ingeld had invented her pregnancy to persuade Ulf to escort her back to Dira.

"Come and see Kazak." Ingeld slipped her arm round Siris's waist.

"Kazak?" Siris knew the name well.

"Yes, he's the supervisor."

She beckoned to them, and led them up the stairs.

Ingeld had changed a great deal since they last saw her. To begin with, her black hair was now beautifully arranged, piled on top of her head, and held in place with a gold circlet. She had also gained weight, so that her figure was now statuesque. She was wearing a gleaming white tunic that showed off her shapely bronzed legs, and white sandals. Her full lips seemed redder than when Niall had last seen her. She was undoubtedly looking prosperous and healthy. By the side of her, Siris looked thin and rather drab.

The next floor was something of a disappointment for a palace. There was simply a wide corridor, with identical wooden doors all the way along. Outside a door at the far end stood two guards whom Niall recognised from the underground city. Instead of giving Niall a friendly smile—as he had expected—they stared woodenly in front of them and straightened their backs as Ingeld went past.

It was the most magnificent room Niall had ever seen. The floor was covered with a royal green carpet, and the walls hung with heavy green curtains. The ceiling was gold, and two immense chandeliers suspended from it sparkled with crystal. There was no furniture, but the floor was covered with cushions. At the far end Kazak was reclining on a pile of these while two women agitated the air around him with fans made of ostrich feathers. A shade of annoyance crossed his face as he saw the strangers who followed Ingeld, then changed to astonishment as he saw

Niall. He started to stand, and the two women hastened to help him.

"My dear boy! This is amazing. Why did no one tell me you were here!" Niall blushed at this effusive welcome. "And can this be Siris? Yes, of course it is! You look just like your sister. Welcome, my dear. Well, well. And you are . . . ?"

"Veig."

"Yes, Veig, of course. And where is . . ." for a moment he tried to recollect the name—"where is Ulf?"

Siris said: "He was killed by the spiders."

Kazak shook his head, and his double chin also shook. "How dreadful! I'm so sorry. Please come and sit down." He turned to one of the women. "Bring us something to drink. Yes, that's right, my dear, sit there." Niall observed the gleam of interest in his eye as he looked at Siris. "Sit down, Niall. And you . . ." He had obviously already forgotten Veig's name. "Yes, I'm so sorry to hear about Ulf. But of course, he killed a spider, didn't he? That's why we're *all* here."

Niall was on the point of telling him the truth, then changed his mind. The less people who knew, the better.

Siris asked: "Where *is* Sefna?"

"She's in the women's quarters. You'll be able to join her later."

"And my children, Runa and Mara—shall I be able to see them?"

"Oh yes, I'm sure that can be arranged."

The girl came back bringing a tray with tall metal cups. The golden drink was sweet and cool, and had a lemony flavour. Kazak's was in a silver cup decorated with precious stones. He said, "Thank you, my dear," and patted the girl's thigh. Then he smiled at Siris. "I drink your health, my dear." Out of the corner of his eye, Niall glimpsed the shade of vexation that crossed Ingeld's face.

Kazak asked: "Who sent you here?"

"A woman dressed in shiny black."

Kazak raised his eyebrows. "One of the servants of the Death Lord. How did you come to meet her?"

"She took us to see him."

Kazak was obviously perplexed. "And you've seen the Great Lord himself? But why?"

Niall let Veig and Siris describe what happened. Kazak listened intently, and his eyes took on a curious, brooding expression. When they had finished, he looked at Niall.

"Do *you* understand what this is all about?"

Niall said awkwardly: "I suppose it's something to do with the killing of the spider."

Kazak asked quickly: "Did he ask you about it?"

"No."

"Then it couldn't be." He gave Niall a penetrating glance from under his hooded lids, and Niall was aware of the force of his personality. "Are you *sure* you've no idea? You can be quite frank with me. You're among friends."

Any impulse Niall had to tell the truth was countered by the same deep impulse that had checked him in the presence of the Spider Lord. He shook his head firmly: "I've no idea."

"Mmmm." Kazak drank meditatively. "Very odd." And for the next ten minutes he questioned them carefully, getting them to describe everything that had happened since they were captured. Niall contented himself with a precise, factual account, but he was aware that Kazak was unsatisfied. The king's intuition told him that the solution of this riddle lay in Niall himself; he could not make up his mind whether Niall was withholding something or not. Again and again, Niall felt the king's penetrating glance trying to pierce through to his secret.

Ingeld was becoming bored and restive. When Kazak paused to sip his drink, she asked: "Shall I take Siris to see the women's quarters?"

Kazak shrugged. "Yes, I suppose so. And you'd better take her to see her children." He smiled at Siris. "It's against the rules, but since it's you . . ."

"But shan't I be allowed to stay with them?" Siris asked.

He shook his head. "Quite impossible, my dear. Ingeld will explain why. But don't fret. I'm sure we can arrange something." He touched her lightly under the chin. "I'll talk to you about it later."

He stood up and escorted them across the room, one hand on Siris's shoulder. At the door he turned to Niall and Veig. "You two will have to work, of course. That's the rule here. Everyone has to work. Even I have to. But you needn't start until tomorrow." He patted them on the shoulder, then turned his back, dismissing them.

In the corridor, Veig asked Ingeld: "What work does he do?"

"Work? He's the king!"

"And they still let him be king, even here?"

"Oh yes. In fact, he's in charge of *all* the people here." She was evidently glad to explain it to them. "As soon as the Spider Lord saw him, he realised that Kazak was exactly what he needed. You see, the people here are so stupid. They need someone to keep them organised."

Niall said: "I thought the commanders did that."

"Yes, but that's the whole point. All the commanders are equal, so they can't appoint one above the others."

"Couldn't they appoint a spider?"

"Oh no, that wouldn't do. To begin with, they don't really understand human beings. And of course, they can't talk." She glanced over her shoulder. "By the way, we're not supposed to call them spiders—they don't like it. We're supposed to refer to them as Masters."

They were crossing the hall downstairs when a woman came in through the door. Niall's heart turned a somersault as he recognized Merlew. Ingeld called to her: "Look who's arrived."

Merlew looked at Niall with pleased astonishment. "Well, it's the young wrestler!" Niall blushed.

Merlew had acquired a suntan. In her short white robe, she looked dazzlingly beautiful. With a sinking of the heart he realised that he found her more alluring than ever. When she gave Veig a warm smile, Niall experienced a pang of jealousy.

Merlew asked: "Where are you going?"

"I'm taking them to the nursery. Why don't you come?"

"No thanks. I've some dressmaking to do. But why not invite them to dinner this evening?"

It was clear that this idea did not appeal to Ingeld. "I'll have to ask your father first."

Merlew said smartly: "Nonsense. *I'm* mistress of this household. I'm inviting them."

Ingeld flushed. "Very well. You can take the responsibility."

"I will." She smiled at them. "I'll see you tonight."

Niall observed the expression on Veig's face as he stared after her. Merlew had made another conquest.

Outside, their charioteer leapt to his feet, but Ingeld surveyed the two-wheeled cart with disfavour. "It looks horribly uncomfortable. I think we'll take ours." She waved dismissively at the charioteer. "You can go." She led them back through the building and out into a paved courtyard. Here two charioteers were sitting in the shade playing the game with carved wooden sticks. When Ingeld snapped her fingers, they leapt to their feet. Niall glimpsed her fleeting smile of pleasure; she evidently enjoyed being able to exhibit her power in front of her relatives.

Niall could see why she preferred her own transport. This two-wheeled cart was large enough for half a dozen, and the seats were comfortably padded. It was made of a light yellow wood, and its wheels were large and elegant. When they were seated, Ingeld said: "To the women's quarters," and the charioteers pulled them out through a rear entrance.

Siris turned to Ingeld. "Do you have to work?"

Ingeld raised her eyebrows. "Oh no. In this city, the men do most of the work. They seem to regard women as a superior species. It's rather pleasant." She smiled complacently at Niall and Veig. "But I wouldn't work anyway. I suppose you might say that I'm the queen."

"You're married to Kazak?"

"Oh no, not exactly. But I'm in charge of his household."

Niall said: "I thought Merlew was."

"We share the work." Her voice was cool.

As they approached the white tower, Niall saw that the main square was swarming with activity. It seemed full of large green insects. He asked Ingeld: "What are they?"

She wrinkled her nose in disgust. "They're the beetles. I can't imagine what they're doing." She leaned forward and asked the charioteers: "Do you know what's going on?"

One of them said: "I should think they're going to 'ave another go at blowin' up the tower."

"Ah. This should be worth watching. Stop where we've got a good view."

They halted at the edge of the square, next to the building that housed the Spider Lord. The square seemed an almost solid mass of green-backed beetles. They had long powerful forelegs, yellow heads and, at the rear, a short, tail-like appendage. They were very large—the largest probably more than six feet long—and their big bodies crashed against one another as they pushed and jostled. When Niall tuned in to their minds, he immediately experienced a sense of effervescent excitement that made him want to laugh aloud. It was totally unlike the watchful vigilance of the spiders, or the strange collective consciousness of the ants. These creatures seemed to be endowed with an excess of high spirits. If they had been human they would have slapped one another on the back and nudged one another in the ribs. As it was, they deliberately bumped against one another out of sheer exuberance.

Some of the black spiders had emerged from the building, but they stayed in the shadow of the portico. Niall sensed in them an attitude of contemptuous dislike for the beetles, mingled with a caution that seemed to contain an element of fear.

At the foot of the white tower, the men had piled barrels in a double row. Then they dragged away the empty carts and pulled them to the far side of the square, where they took up positions behind them. Only the little man in the yellow tunic was left near the tower. He picked up a small barrel and proceeded to lay a powder trail across the turf, halting at the low wall that divided the grass surrounding the tower from the main square. The beetles suddenly became still as the man struck a light with a tinder box; a moment later, a wisp of white smoke rose from the end of the powder trail and raced across the grass. The little man lay down behind the wall, and covered his ears with his hands. Something about the tension in his arms aroused in Niall an intuition of danger. He grabbed Veig and Siris by the arm.

"Quick!"

They responded to the urgency in his voice and followed him as he scrambled out of the cart. Ingeld hesitated, perhaps feeling that it would be beneath her dignity to hurry, but finally followed them. As her foot touched the ground, there was a crashing roar like a thousand thunder-claps and a blinding burst of light. A moment later, Niall felt himself caught by a tremendous wind that threw him backwards. Fortunately, the cart took most of the blast and was turned over on its side. Niall's skull exploded into stars as he was spun and thrown against the wall of the building. Something struck him in the back and knocked the breath out of his lungs. When his vision cleared, he saw that it was Veig, who was now sprawling on the ground. Siris lay a few feet away. Ingeld, caught upright by the blast, and without the shelter of the cart, had been hurled twenty feet into the middle of the avenue. So were the two charioteers. The white tower was blackened but obviously undamaged.

There was chaos in the square, a struggling mass of beetles, many upside down, their legs waving in the air. Some of them had been picked up by the blast and hurled against the wall of the building behind them, where they had landed on top of the spiders.

The air was full of a horrible, pungent stench that made him cough and brought tears to his eyes. It took him a few moments to realise that the source of these choking fumes was not the explosion but the beetles themselves. One of the black spiders, trying to drag itself out from under the body of a struggling beetle, struck out with its fangs, which glanced off the green armour plating. There was the sound of an explosion, and the spider was instantly surrounded by a cloud of poisonous green gas discharged from the beetle's tail-like appendage. They were close enough for Niall to feel the heat that accompanied the cloud. The spider dragged itself clear, leaving behind the end segment of one of its legs, and hastened to remove itself from the vicinity of the choking fumes.

As order was restored, it became clear that no one had been badly hurt. Ingeld was standing up, her white tunic torn and stained with blood; but when Niall ran to help her, he discovered that the blood came from a nosebleed; her cheek was scratched, and so were her hands and knees; otherwise she seemed undamaged. Veig and Siris looked dazed, but were unhurt. The charioteers had been less fortunate; one had done a somersault over the cart and seemed to have a broken leg; the other was bleeding from a dozen cuts on his head and shoulders. Niall's intuition of danger had been sound. If they had remained in the cart, they would have been picked up and hurled backwards. Now he understood why the men had dragged their own carts so far across the square.

The little man in the yellow tunic was making his way towards them. Niall saw that it was Bill Doggins and that he was avoiding the jostling of the beetles with a skill that suggested long practice. Ingeld rushed at him screaming "Idiot!" then doubled up with coughing.

"Sorry about that," he said.

"What happened?" Niall asked.

"We used a bit too much gunpowder, that's what. Mind, it wasn't my fault. Orders from 'is 'ighness 'imself." He nodded in the direction of the headquarters of the Death Lord.

Ingeld, who was still choking, gasped: "You're a dangerous lunatic. I'm going to report you to the king."

The little man shrugged. "Report me to who you like."

She glowered at him. "I will." She turned to Siris. "I'm going back to change." She walked away with a slight limp.

Siris hardly seemed to notice her departure; she was regarding the little man with an expression of awe.

"How do you do it? Are you a magician?"

He snorted with laughter. "I wouldn't say that. I'm what

used to be called a sapper. That's someone who blows things up." He held out his hand. "My name's Bill Doggins, by the way. What's yours?"

When the introductions were over, Doggins said: "Ah well, better get on with the job. Let's go and see if we've managed to knock a few chips off it."

They followed him across the grass. His workmen had already gathered round the foot of the tower. He called: "Any luck?"

One of the men shook his head. "Not a bloody crack." He dipped a cloth in a bucket of water and wiped it across the black soot left by the explosion. "Just look at that!" The wet cloth left a spotlessly white mark behind it. "It hasn't even stuck to it!"

At close quarters, Niall could see that the tower was not pure white; there was a slight tinge of blue-grey which may have been due to the fact that it seemed partly transparent. To stare at it was a strange sensation, a little like staring into deep water. Niall felt that his eyes should be able to see through its surface, if only he tried hard enough; yet the harder he tried, the more he became aware of the reflection of his own face looking back at him. The effort seemed to make him slightly dizzy. He was reminded of the occasion when his father had taught him to dowse for water with a forked twig; at a certain point, the twig had writhed in his hand, as if it had suddenly come to life, and he had experienced this same curious dizziness as if falling slowly into a deep pit.

He reached out and wiped the black gunpowder stain with his finger; it came off on his fingertip, leaving the surface smooth and shiny. But he noticed the faint electrical tingle as he touched the tower. He pressed the flat of his hand against the spot that had already been wiped clean and the sensation seemed stronger. At the same time, he experienced an indescribable sensation in his head. It was like smelling some sharp, metallic odour, completely unlike the sulphurous smell the gunpowder had left behind. It happened again when he pressed his hand against the surface a second time, and was even stronger when he used both hands.

Doggins was staring up towards the top of the tower, his face twisted into a grimace of puzzlement.

"Why'd you suppose they built it if they don't want anybody to get inside?"

Veig said: "Perhaps it's solid."

Doggins looked at Niall. "Do *you* think so?"

Niall thought about it, then shook his head.

"No, do you?"

"No."

"Why not?"

Doggins shrugged. "Same reason as you. I just don't."

A number of bombardier beetles had joined them. Niall could sense their disappointment as they searched the white surface for any trace of a crack. One approached Doggins, and seemed to be rubbing its feelers together. To Niall's surprise, Doggin's raised his hands in front of his face and made similar movements with his fingers, occasionally touching both hands together. The beetle made more movements with its feelers.

Veig whispered incredulously: "I think they're talking."

Doggins, who overheard the remark, grinned. "Of course we're talking." He made more signals with his fingers. The beetle replied, then turned and walked away. For a creature of such size, it moved with remarkable lightness.

Niall asked: "What was he saying?"

"He says we ought to dig a trench round the foot of the tower and try to get the gunpowder underneath it."

Siris said: "But why do they want to blow it up? It's so beautiful."

"*They* don't care one way or the other. It's them bleedin' crawlies who want to blow it up."

"But why?"

Doggins sighed. "I dunno. They just don't like anything they can't understand." He glanced sideways at a number of death spiders who, together with a group of commanders, were approaching the tower. "But I don't think they're going to succeed. Not with gunpowder anyway. Now if we could get hold of a bit of dynamite or TNT . . ."

Niall walked slowly round the tower, peering hard at its surface, trying to detect any sign of an entrance. There was not even a crack in the smooth alabaster surface. He continued to experience a curious, tingling sensation, and a sharp, metallic odour.

A voice behind him said: "What are you doing here?"

He started as if awakened from a dream. Odina was standing so close that he bumped into her as he turned.

"I . . . we're . . . looking at the tower."

"You know it is forbidden for servants to approach it?"

"No, I didn't."

"Well, it is. And in this city, ignorance is no excuse. If it happens again you will be punished."

"I'm sorry."

Her stern gaze softened. "What are you doing here? Why are you not working?"

"King Kazak said we could start tomorrow."

"King Kazak?" For a moment she was puzzled. "Ah, the new supervisor. Well, he is subject to the law, like the rest of us. Idleness is against the law."

Niall said: "We were on our way to see the women's quarters and nursery. But our guide was hurt by the explosion."

"Wait here."

She left him and went back to the group of commanders who were peering into the crater left by the explosion. She talked earnestly for a while, and several of the women glanced curiously at Niall, then at Siris and Veig. After a few minutes she returned.

"Come, I will escort you." She went up to Veig, who was talking to Doggins, and tapped him briskly on the shoulder.

"Follow me."

He was startled, but obeyed her. As Siris turned to follow, Doggins gave her a solemn wink.

Odina shook her head at Veig. "Servants are not allowed to speak to slaves of the beetles."

"Why not?"

The question seemed to irritate her. "Because that is the law. We must all obey the law. And servants are not allowed to ask questions."

"I'm sorry."

His apology seemed to mollify her. She beckoned imperiously to a group of charioteers sitting on the wall that surrounded the square; they all snapped to attention. "Take us to the women's quarters." Four men pulled a cart over to them and stood at attention as they climbed in. It was only just large enough for four, and Veig and Niall were squeezed on either side of Odina. Niall found the contact of bare arms and thighs curiously disturbing. He observed that, under her bronzed sun tan, Odina's face had coloured.

THE CHARIOTEERS took a side street out of the square. The buildings towered above them, cutting out the sunlight.

Odina said: "You may ask me questions."

Veig, who disliked taking orders, replied: "But you told us we weren't to ask questions."

"I have now given you permission." Her voice was as wooden as her expression.

There was silence as they tried to think of something to ask. Then Siris spoke:

"Who built this city?"

"I cannot answer that question."

Veig said: "Why aren't we allowed to speak to the servants of the beetles?"

"I cannot answer that question."

Niall said: "Where is the great happy land?"

"I cannot answer that question."

"Because you don't know the answer, or because you're not allowed to tell us?" Veig asked.

"Because I don't know the answer."

Niall said: "*What* is the great happy land?"

"It is a land over the sea where the faithful servants of the masters go to live out their lives in peace."

Niall said: "Can I ask you another question?"

"Yes."

"Last night, when I called the masters 'spiders,' you told me not to use that word or I'd find myself in the great happy land. What did you mean?"

She smiled. "We also use it to denote the land where the soul goes after death."

Veig said: "But the servants don't have to die before they can go there?"

She looked scandalised. "Of course not! They go there as a reward for faithful service."

The cart had crossed two broad avenues. Ahead, the street now seemed to be blocked by a high wall. Then, as they came closer, Niall realised that the wall ran down the centre of an avenue. At close quarters it was impressive: enormous carved grey blocks, each more than two feet long and cut so accurately that no mortar was required to hold them together. A row of iron spikes ran along the top. A few hundred yards along the avenue, the wall was pierced by a small gateway, the iron gate closed. Two wolf spiders stood on either side of it. As they approached, a woman in a black commander's uniform came out of a small stone building beside the gate. Odina called:

"These are newly arrived prisoners. I am taking the woman to her quarters."

The commander glared at Niall and Veig with obvious contempt. "Then why are the men going too?"

"They are her sons. They are going to visit their sisters in the nursery."

The woman shrugged and unlocked the gate with a huge

iron key, then stood aside to allow them through. Niall and Veig kept their eyes averted from her scornful gaze. Niall asked Odina:

"Why did she seem so angry?" He meant "bad tempered" but felt it would be tactless to say so.

"Men are not allowed in this part of the city. To be caught here without permission means death."

The streets here seemed totally deserted. There were no platoons of slaves, no wolf spiders, no charioteers waiting for passengers. Even the spider webs stretched across the streets seemed dusty and old, as if abandoned long ago. Many of the windows were broken, and they could see through into empty rooms whose walls were often in a state of collapse.

At the end of another long, narrow street, they emerged suddenly into a large square. In its centre was a tall column surrounded by lawns and flower beds. After the uniform grey of the buildings, the colours were dazzling. Odina said:

"This is where the women live."

The buildings that surrounded the square were all in an excellent state of preservation; their windows gleamed in the sunlight. Many of them had impressive columns in front of the main door. On a lawn at the far end of the square, a group of women were being drilled by a commander clad in black. Other women, dressed in identical white tunics, were kneeling in the flowerbeds or pushing barrows. Odina pointed to a building with a pink façade.

"That is the hostel for newly arrived women prisoners." She tapped one of the charioteers on the shoulder. "Stop here." She explained to Niall and Veig: "Men are not allowed to approach within a hundred paces on pain of death." The cart halted in the middle of the square. She and

Siris climbed out. Niall watched them cross the lawn and disappear into the pink building.

The charioteers stood at attention, holding the shafts of the cart. Niall and Veig sat there in the sunshine, staring with appreciation at the flower beds. He had never seen so many colours in such proximity: reds and purples, blues and yellows, all surrounded by the soothing green of the lawns. There were also bushes, many covered with tiny red flowers, or with magnificent purple blossoms.

They soon realised that they were also an object of curiosity. Women broke off their work to stare at them. Then a tall blonde woman who had been working nearby, trimming the edges of the grass with a small sickle, came over to them. Niall smiled at her and said hello, but she ignored him. She was looking with interest at Veig. Then she reached out and felt the muscles of his upper arm. Veig blushed. The woman smiled at him invitingly, then reached up and touched his cheek.

Niall became aware that a girl standing by the edge of the flower bed was signalling to him. When he stared at her, she beckoned imperiously and called: "Slave!" When Niall pointed to himself, she nodded, and again beckoned to him. Niall looked towards the charioteers for advice, but they were staring straight ahead. Finally, since the girl seemed to be growing impatient, Niall climbed out of the cart and went across to her. She was a pretty, dark-haired girl with a snub nose and firm chin; something about her reminded him of Merlew.

"What is your name?" she demanded.

"Niall."

"Come here, Niall." The girl turned and walked away from him. Slightly mystified, he followed her towards the bushes that formed the centerpiece of the flower bed. When they were within their shade she turned to him and said imperiously: "Kiss me."

Niall gaped; it was the last thing he had expected. The girl grew tired of his hesitation, pulled him towards her and wound her arms round his neck. A moment later, her body was pressed tightly against his own while her lips kissed him swiftly and repeatedly. After his initial surprise, Niall found the sensation delicious, and abandoned himself to its pleasure.

After a few moments, the girl gave a sigh of delight and drew back to look at him. "Now kiss me," she said. Niall obeyed without hesitation. The soft lips parted, and she placed both her hands behind his head to hold their faces together. They clung together for so long that he became slightly breathless.

The girl pulled away from him, gently released herself, and peeped round the edge of the bush. Satisfied that they were unobserved, she took him by the hand and said: "Come over here." Her voice was trembling and breathless. Niall allowed her to lead him to a patch of long, unmown grass. She dropped down in it and held out her arms. Niall was puzzled. He could see no advantage in kissing horizontally rather than vertically. Nevertheless, he obeyed, and allowed himself to be pulled down beside her. A moment later, her hands were once again locked behind his head, while her lips moved so urgently against his own he felt as if she were drinking him.

A tremendous blow on the ear made his head explode with light. He looked up and saw Odina bending over them, prepared to hit him again. His head ringing, he scrambled to his feet. Odina's eyes were blazing with anger. She gave the girl a violent kick with her boot. "Get up, you slut." She turned on Niall, and he had to dodge another blow.

The girl seemed quite unafraid; the main expression on

her face was of regret. When Odina drew back her foot to kick her again, a dangerous expression came into her eyes, and Odina changed her mind.

"Get back to work! I'll deal with you later." She turned on Niall. "You, get back in the cart."

The cart was empty; the four men at the shafts looking stolidly ahead, like patient horses. Odina strode past them, into the clump of flowering shrubs in the centre of the next flowerbed. Niall considered whether to shout a warning to his brother, then remembered Odina's furious eyes and decided against it. There was a cry of pain, and a few moments later, Odina stormed out of the shrubbery, dragging Veig by the ear. Niall could not prevent himself from laughing, but an angry glare from Odina checked his mirth. The blonde woman followed them, looking cowed. Odina pointed silently to the cart. Veig came and joined Niall there. Without giving them another glance, Odina strode back into the pink-fronted building. The women went on with their work as if nothing had happened. From the far end of the square, they could hear the sound of feet marching in unison.

Veig said: "Do you think she is very angry?"

"She looks furious. But it wasn't my fault. I thought that girl wanted to show me something."

Veig chuckled: "She did."

A quarter of an hour went past. Finally, Odina came back, followed by Siris. She snapped an order at the charioteers, and they launched into simultaneous motion. Odina looked from Veig to Niall, but they avoided her gaze. She said:

"You're lucky it was me and not some other commander. The penalty for unlawful bundling is fifty lashes."

"Bundling?"

Siris was mystified. "What have you been doing?"

"She asked me to help her move a heavy wheelbarrow," Veig said. "When we got into the bushes, she leapt on me. I thought she was going to eat me."

Odina looked sternly at Niall. "I suppose that dark haired girl asked *you* to go and help her?"

"No. She did this with her finger, and I went to see what she wanted."

"You're a couple of fools. Don't you realise that the women's section is forbidden territory to men? If I reported this you'd lose both your ears." But her tone had a note of protectiveness.

Niall said: "But what's wrong with kissing? Why is it against the law?"

Odina took a deep breath; for a moment, it looked as if she might get angry again. Then she shook her head pityingly.

"You have much to learn. There is nothing wrong with kissing, provided the right people are doing it. But sometimes the wrong people do it."

"Who *are* the wrong people?"

"Have you seen any of the slaves yet?"

"Yes, we passed some of them this morning."

"You saw how horrible they looked?"

"Yes."

"That is because their parents were the wrong people. You see how strong and healthy I am?" She stretched out her shapely arm and flexed the muscle.

"Yes."

"That is because my parents were the right people." She smiled at them with genuine kindness, as if she had explained everything.

They absorbed this in silence for a moment. Then Niall asked: "What sort of people *were* your parents."

She looked surprised. "I don't know."

They all stared at her in astonishment. "You don't know?"

"Of course not."

Niall said: "But I know who my parents are."

Odina nodded. "But you are savages. You leave reproduction and breeding to chance. Why do you suppose all the commanders look so strong and healthy? Because their parents were carefully chosen. Why are all our men so tall and handsome? Because we do not leave their breeding to chance."

"But are *all* your babies born strong and healthy?" Siris asked.

"Of course not. But if they are weak and unhealthy, they are not allowed to live."

Siris asked mildly: "Isn't that rather cruel?"

"No. It would be cruel if we let them live, for their children might also be unhealthy. By not allowing them to live, we make sure that our whole race remains strong and healthy."

Veig asked: "But what about the slaves?"

"The slaves are an inferior class. We keep them because we need someone to do the unpleasant jobs. And of course, the spiders . . ." she quickly corrected herself, "the masters need them for their banquets."

Niall asked, with misgivings: "As servants?"

"No. No." She seemed mildly impatient. "As the main dish. They love human flesh. Of course, we also breed cows and horses and sheeps. But they say human flesh tastes best of all."

This left them feeling slightly shaken. After a long pause, Veig asked: "Doesn't that . . . worry you?"

She shook her head vigorously. "Of course not. They never eat their servants—unless, of course, they go out after dark. Or break the law in some other way. Like trying to get into the women's section." She said this with a note of warning, glancing at them from under lowered eyelids.

For the past ten minutes, the cart had been travelling along the same broad avenue in the direction of the river; now, as the charioteers struggled to prevent the cart from running away on a downhill slope, it lay directly ahead of them, a wide expanse of water glittering in the sunlight. The immense bridge that had once arched across it was not broken in the middle; the rusty iron girders were twisted and bent. The charioteers were ordered to halt. Odina pointed to a low white building on the other side of the water.

"There is the nursery."

Siris asked anxiously: "But how can we get across?"

For answer, Odina pointed to a boat that lay on the foreshore at the bottom of a flight of steps. She tapped two of the charioteers on the shoulder. "You can take us across. You two wait here."

A few minutes later, they were in the middle of the river; the boat, which was like a smaller version of a Viking craft, shot forward smoothly with every stroke of the oars.

Niall asked: "How did the bridge become broken?"

"The servants of the beetles blew it up. It is to prevent the mothers from trying to see their children."

Siris asked: "But aren't the mothers *ever* allowed to see their children?"

"Of course, twice a year. Then, if they wish, they can spend a whole day together. But of course, many of them prefer not to bother. I have not seen my own children since birth."

"*You* have children?"

She corrected her. "I have borne children, I do not have them."

Siris asked: "But didn't you want to see them?"

She shrugged. "I missed them a little for the first week, then the feeling went away. I knew they were well cared for."

"And who is your . . . who is their father?" Siris asked.

"One was called Brucis, one was called Mardak, and one was called Kryphon."

She asked timidly: "And . . . do you still see them?"

Odina sighed; she obviously found Siris's questions naïve. "I have passed them occasionally in the street. But it would be impolite to show that we knew each other. You see, they are only servants. Their business is to father children. They would be embarrassed if I spoke to them."

"But don't you *feel* anything for them?"

"Why should I? Would you expect me to feel something for these men"—she gestured at the charioteers—"because they are rowing us across the river?"

Niall glanced cautiously at the two men, wondering whether they might be upset by her remark; but they were staring straight ahead and showed no sign of having heard.

The boat bumped to a halt against a flight of steps; one of the men leapt out and secured it to a ring, then helped Odina to step ashore.

At the top of the steps they encountered a tall, powerfully-built woman dressed entirely in blue; like most of the commanders, she resembled Odina so much that she might have been her sister. She was carrying an axe that was taller than she was; a spike protruded from the back of the blade. She saluted Odina, then glanced down at Siris's stomach.

"How many months?"

"She is not pregnant," Odina said. "She is here to visit her children, who arrived a few days ago."

The woman said: "I hope you can control her." She stood to attention as they went past.

"What did she mean?" Siris asked in a whisper.

Odina shrugged. "Some of the mothers refuse to leave their children. Only last week, she had to kill one of them."

"Kill her!"

"Yes, she had to chop off her head."

Veig said: "Couldn't she just have knocked her unconscious?"

Odina shook her head decisively. "No. She was suffering from emotional disease. She might have infected others."

"Emotional disease?"

"That is what we call it when people refuse to control themselves. And of course, such a woman might produce tainted children. That is why they must be killed."

They were crossing a pleasant lawn, with a large flowerbed. Ahead was a long, white building, its windows shielded by brightly coloured awnings. Many women in various states of pregnancy wandered about the lawns, or sat in the shade of trees. A few women in blue uniforms could also be seen; each of these carried a small hand axe suspended from her belt.

Odina pointed to a wooden bench on the edge of the lawn. "You two will have to wait there. No men are allowed in the children's quarters. But make sure you stay there until we come back. The guards have orders to kill any man who wanders around here without permission."

Niall and Veig sat on the sun-warmed bench—it was, in fact, uncomfortably hot—and watched Siris and Odina disappear round the corner of the building. Niall could hear a strange hissing sound, and the trickle of running water; by leaning backwards and peering around an intervening tree, he could see a fountain that hurled a spray of water high into the air. It fascinated him, and he would have liked to go and investigate; but one of the women in blue was standing on the edge of the lawn and eyeing them with an open disapproval that made him nervous. He could imagine her severing his head with one fierce swing of the axe.

"What do you think about all this?" Veig indicated the women and the nursery buildings.

"It's very beautiful." To the eye of a desert dweller, it might have been the Garden of Eden.

"It's beautiful, but it makes me shiver. It's like that woman who brought us here . . ."

"What do you mean?"

"She's so pretty, and she seems so nice, yet she says such horrible things. I felt quite sick when she told us about that woman having her head chopped off—just for wanting to stay with her baby."

"Sshh!"Niall said. He suspected they could be overheard by the woman in blue and that Odina might return to find two headless bodies.

"I don't see why I *should* be quiet." Nevertheless Veig lowered his voice.

Niall said: "I'll tell you what puzzles me. If they go to so much trouble to make sure the babies are all strong and healthy, why are they all so *stupid*?"

Veig was struck by this. "Yes, you're right. They *are* stupid, aren't they?" He thought about it. "Perhaps it's because their jobs are all so boring."

Niall shook his head. "No, it's more than that. I've got a feeling . . ."

Before he could put it into words they were interrupted by an excited shout; a moment later, Runa had flung her arms round them and was trying to hug and kiss them both at the same time. Behind her came Siris, carrying Mara. And behind Siris, walking with Odina, was a slim girl dressed in a blue tunic. To his delight, Niall recognised Dona. He freed himself from Runa and jumped to his feet; Dona ran towards him, holding out her hands. Her eyes were shining with excitement. Niall hugged her round the waist and swung her round, lifting her feet off the ground. This was too much for the blue-clad guard, who stepped forward angrily and said:

"That's enough of this bundling! If you're not careful, you'll both lose your ears."

Niall put her down guiltily, and Dona turned away, abashed. Then, to Niall's surprise, Odina said:

"You're quite right, commander. But these people are savages who haven't seen one another for a long time. I'll make sure they behave themselves." She gave her a winning smile. The guard shrugged ill-humouredly and turned away.

"I'll bundle you later when there's no one around," Niall whispered to Dona.

She blushed rosily, and Niall's heart turned a somersault. In the semi-darkness of Kazak's underground city, he had never noticed how pretty she was. In the months since he had last seen her, the thin child's body had filled out, and the shapely arms and shoulders were tanned.

Runa and Mara also looked sunburned and healthy; and both were distinctly plumper. When Runa asked "Where's daddy?" Niall realised that she was unaware of her father's death. Fortunately, Mara changed the subject by asking Veig to tell her a story. Niall and Dona sat at the end of the bench and looked at each other. He felt grateful to Odina when she wandered across the lawn to talk to the guard.

"Why are you wearing that blue dress?" he asked.

"I'm one of the nursemaids. I help take care of the children. I've been given Runa and Mara to look after."

"Do you like it here?"

"Oh yes, I love the children. But it's a bit lonely without mummy."

"I'm going to see Kazak tonight. Would you like me to

ask him if you could go and work for him? He lives in a beautiful palace."

Her eyes lit up for a moment. "Will you be there?"

"No. I have to start to work tomorrow."

Her face became sad. They looked at each other and realised that it might be a long time before they met again. Suddenly, he wanted more than anything in the world to hug and kiss her. Looking into her eyes, he was aware that she shared his desire. But in the presence of the guard—who kept glancing suspiciously towards them—it was impossible. Instead, they cautiously allowed their hands to touch.

Niall was interested to observe how far their minds seemed to be in tune. He was not making any conscious effort to read her thoughts, yet was as aware of them as if they were inside his own head. It was as if, in the excitement of rediscovering one another, their mental lives were interpenetrating.

The guard changed her position so she could observe them over Odina's shoulder. Curious to know the cause of her hostility, Niall tried tuning in to her mind. It was unexpectedly difficult, and for a moment Niall suspected that she was aware of his efforts, and was deliberately blocking them. Yet her face, as she listened to Odina, seemed to betray no such awareness. He tried again, and was suddenly struck by a strange suspicion: that the woman's mind was inaccessible because it was not functioning on the normal human level. A moment later, his efforts succeeded, and he realised with a shock that he had been correct. This was not the blankness he had observed so often in the inhabitants of the spider city, which was almost a form of absent-mindedness. This was the strange, watchful passivity of a spider waiting for its prey to fly into the web. Incredible as it seemed, he was looking at a human being whose mind functioned like that of a spider.

Dona, he noticed, was looking at him curiously, aware that something unusual was taking place. Yet because their minds were in harmony, she made no attempt to gain his attention; she was curious to know what was fascinating him so much.

Now, suddenly, Niall could see exactly why the guard was watching them with so much hostility. She detested savages, regarding them with contemptuous superiority. The sight of Niall and Veig filled her with antagonism. But Odina was her superior in rank; so unless Niall or Veig broke the rules, she had no right to object. The force of her dislike was so strong that Niall felt himself colouring with anger.

She seemed totally unaware that Niall was observing her mind. Something about her attitude reminded him of the tent spider, although the force of her vitality was far stronger. Impelled partly by malice, partly by curiosity, Niall tried the experiment of implanting an idea in her mind; he tried to make her feel that someone was staring at her out of a window of the nursery building. For a few seconds, nothing happened; the woman continued to listen to Odina, nodding her head and keeping Niall and Dona under observation. Then, as if she could stand it no longer, she turned abruptly and stared towards the nursery. Niall was astonished by the success of his experiment. He tried willing her to raise her hand and scratch her nose. This time she obeyed without hesitation. Niall found it almost unbelievable. She was obeying his will without even being aware of it. He made her shift from one foot to the other, fiddle with the axe at her belt, reach round to scratch the small of her back. Finally, he made her look intently towards the nursery building, trying to identify the source of her vague discomfort. While she did this, he took the opportunity to lean forward and snatch a kiss from Dona. When the guard looked back again, they had just separated.

A few minutes later, Odina turned and made a signal to Dona. It had evidently been prearranged.

"I have to go now," Dona whispered. "I've got to distract your sisters so they won't cry when you go." She glanced round to make sure the guard was looking the other way, then reached up and briefly caressed Niall's cheek. Then she stood up and took Mara by the hand. "How about a game of hide and seek? Come on—you and Runa run and hide, and I'll come and find you."

A moment later, Runa and Mara were almost out of sight among the bushes and Odina signalled that it was time to leave. Niall tried to catch Dona's eye for the last time, but she was already hurrying away across the lawn.

As he climbed back into the boat, Niall's mind was a seething ferment of questions and insights. Unaccustomed to sustained rational thinking, he felt as if his head was going to burst.

One thing seemed very clear. The nursery guard was not a spider; she was a human being. So if her mind resembled that of a spider, it must be because it had been shaped and moulded by the spiders—moulded from such an early age that it had taken the imprint of the spider mentality. After all, Veig had "moulded" the pepsis wasp and the ants until they were, in some respects, almost human . . .

This seemed to explain how the spiders controlled their servants. Unlike the bombardier beetles, they seemed to have no obvious form of communication. That was because it was unnecessary; they merely had to implant an idea, a suggestion. Every one of the servants of the Death Lord contained a "second self;" and that second self was a spider . . .

So long as the spiders controlled this second self, they

were the undisputed masters of their human slaves. But what they had not anticipated was that another human mind might take advantage of their training and achieve direct control of their slaves.

And now, for the first time, Niall was suddenly aware of why the Death Lord was so anxious to uncover his secret. If human beings could master the techniques of mind control, then the days of spider supremacy were numbered. Like a tame insect, the slave-mind was a lock that could be opened by more than one key.

As these thoughts struggled to find expression in words, Niall was studying Odina. Compared to the nursery guard, she was indisputably a true human being. Yet even in her, Niall could detect that curious blankness, as if a part of her mind had been put to sleep. That blankness, he now recognised, was a sign that her mind had been violated by the spiders. Her mental privacy had been stolen, and she was not even aware of it.

At the moment, for example, she was wondering what to do with the "savages." Her present situation made her vaguely unhappy. She was accustomed to living her days according to a strict routine. Although the routine varied, its rules were inflexible; for every problem, the rules had an answer. But now she was not sure which of the rules applied. She had offered to take charge of the savages because it was obviously incorrect for them to be wandering around alone. Now she had done her duty, she was not sure what to do next. At the moment, she intended to take Siris back to the women's quarters. But that would still leave the problem of what to do with Veig and Niall . . .

The thought of being separated from his mother made Niall decide to try to implant a suggestion in Odina's mind. The boat was close to the opposite shore; time was running short. He stared at her profile, and concentrated on the suggestion that she should take them all back to Kazak's palace. It was hard to assess her reaction. As the prow of the boat gently nudged the bank, he asked: "Where are we going now?"

"I'm taking you back to the new supervisor." Her voice was clear and decisive. He could sense that she was pleased with herself for thinking of this convenient solution. It made him feel guilty, but when he looked at his mother's sad face—she was still thinking of her children—the guilt was outweighed by satisfaction at winning her this temporary reprieve.

It was mid-afternoon when they arrived back in the main square. Niall felt sorry for the charioteers; Odina had ordered them to return via a lengthy detour along the river bank, and they were exhausted. She seemed completely indifferent to their misery, and often shouted at them to go faster. It occurred to Niall that this was not a matter of cruelty or callousness; her imagination simply failed to grasp them as fellow creatures. This was what disturbed him about her; she seemed pleasant, kindly and well meaning, yet she was totally devoid of imagination.

A group of slaves was pulling a cartload of earth across the square, while others pushed behind. At the foot of the tower, more slaves were filling in the crater. Among these were a number of men whose size and muscular development proclaimed them servants rather than members of the slave class. Niall asked:

"Why are those men working with the slaves?"

"They are being punished. Servants who are disobedient or lazy can be sentenced to become slaves." She added with satisfaction: "It is one of the best ways of maintaining discipline. Most servants would die rather than become slaves."

Veig asked: "Does that mean they might be eaten?"

"Of course. They lose all their privileges."

"What kind of disobedience?"

She shrugged. "Failing to show proper respect to a commander. Even staying in bed too long in the mornings."

Now Niall understood why Massig had been so nervous this morning.

Two black-clad commanders were standing on guard at the main entrance of Kazak's headquarters. Behind them, through the open door, Niall caught a glimpse of a death spider. His heart contracted with sudden apprehension as their charioteers turned into the side street and took the rear entrance that led into the courtyard. Two wolf spiders were lounging in the sun, and two more commanders stood on either side of the entrance to the building. Odina climbed out of the cart, made an obeisance to the spiders, and saluted the commanders.

"I am delivering the savages back to Supervisor Kazak."

The woman stared contemptuously at Niall and Veig.

"I will inform the supervisor. Leave them here."

Odina saluted, climbed back into the cart, and barked an order at the charioteers. She left without a backward glance.

The commander kept them waiting for ten minutes, ignoring them as though they were invisible. Staring at her, Niall found himself tuning in naturally to her emotional vibrations. What he saw made him flush with anger. She regarded "savages" as a contemptible form of animal life, and was convinced they had an unpleasant smell. But most of her contempt was reserved for Siris, whom she saw as repulsively skinny and unfeminine. For a moment, Niall actually saw his mother through her eyes; it was a disturbing experience, as if Siris had been physically transformed into a kind of ape.

From somewhere inside the building, a door slammed

and a woman's voice shouted an order. Their guard turned and vanished into the building. She was away for about ten minutes. The other guard gazed stolidly in front of her; her way of overcoming her disgust towards savages was to try to pretend they were not there.

The door opened; the guard snapped: "Follow me."

Even before he entered, Niall sensed the hostility that awaited him inside. What he had not expected was to find the hall full of black death spiders, so many that there was scarcely room to move between them. Niall had to fight a powerful urge to turn and run. The nearest spiders were watching him as if ready to pounce and sink their fangs into his bare flesh. For a brief moment of panic, he felt the end had come, and tensed himself to fight. But the impenetrable black eyes merely watched as he followed the guard. He could sense in them a mixture of fear and loathing, as if he were some noxious poison insect. With a detached part of his mind, he also noted that this battery of hostile will-power produced an actual sensation of physical cold, like an icy wind. When he followed the guard up the stairs, it was confined to his back. As they turned the corner, it vanished. It was impossible to doubt that the gaze of the spiders carried some negative charge.

They passed the corridor leading to Kazak's chamber and continued up the stairs; after the fourth floor, these became narrower, and Niall realised they were being taken to the top of the building. At the end of every corridor, wolf spiders stood on guard, although this part of the building seemed deserted. It was in a poor state of repair; the walls were disfigured by black and green mould, and slabs of plaster had fallen off, exposing the lath underneath.

They turned into a badly-lit corridor whose wooden floor creaked and yielded ominously under their feet. The guard opened a door and beckoned to Siris.

"You will remain in there until you are needed."

The room inside seemed to be bare, except for a bed and a wooden chair. Siris said "Thank you." Her lips were very pale. The guard slammed the door behind her and pushed a bolt into place.

Two doors farther along, she beckoned to Veig, and pointed. The door was bolted behind him.

Niall was taken to the far end of the corridor. The door was already open. She gestured for him to enter. He asked:

"Are we prisoners?"

"You will speak only when you are spoken to." She stood back as he went in as if to avoid contamination from the slightest contact. The door slammed and the bolt slid into place. He heard her footsteps retreating over the creaking boards.

This room was so badly lit that it took him a few moments to see that it was entirely bare except for a few cushions scattered on the floor. There was a smell of dust and decay. The only light came from a high window which was opaque with grime.

He bent down and picked up a cushion. It was damp and smelt of mould. Quite suddenly, he felt an overwhelming desire to fling himself on the floor and burst into tears. Ever since he had discovered the bloated body of his father, Niall had carried a burden of misery; now it seemed to rise up inside him like a storm, sweeping away all attempts at resistance. Yet some final remnant of pride held him back from his surrender. He sat down in a corner on the damp cushion, pressing his forehead against his knees. At that moment he felt more alone than he had ever been in his life.

Only one explanation seemed to fit the facts: that they had somehow discovered that he was responsible for the death of the spider in the desert. In that case, there could be only one outcome: public execution for all three of them . . . The thought of bringing so much misery on his mother and Veig made him feel like groaning aloud.

But how could they have discovered his secret? He could imagine only one possibility: that he had been betrayed by the expanding metal spear. He had wiped it carefully afterwards, to remove all traces of the spider's blood. But it might still be detectable by senses keener than his own. He cursed his own stupidity for bringing the spear with him instead of leaving it behind in the burrow.

A curious feeling of being observed made him look up and stare intently towards the door. It was made of wooden planks and looked solid enough to withstand a battering ram. When he examined it more closely, there was no sign of any crack or chink through which he might be watched. He decided that his nerves were playing him tricks and sat down again. But whenever he closed his eyes, resting his forehead on his knees, the uncomfortable sense of being observed persisted. If he leaned his head back against the wall and looked straight at the door, it seemed to vanish.

Time seemed to hang in suspension. His mind slipped into a dull passivity; occasionally, his eyelids drooped and he was jerked into wakefulness as his head slid sideways. He felt that time had come to a halt. After what seemed a very long time—perhaps two hours—a faint sound made him alert. It was the squeak of a door. He listened intently, but heard nothing more. Finally, after another long silence, he heard the creak of a floorboard. He crossed to the door and placed his ear against it. There was no further sound.

That could mean only one thing: it was not a human being who had retreated along the corridor. In that silence, any human being, no matter how light, would have been audible. But a spider, with its wide leg span, could tread on the solid boards on either sides of the corridor. The creak of the door indicated that it had been in the next room.

Now, suddenly, he understood that feeling of being observed. It was not of eyes watching him through some crack in the door, but of a mind tuning in to his own. Because of his fatigue and despair, he had made no attempt to shield his thoughts. He cast his mind back, trying to recall every mood and thought since he had heard the guard's retreating footsteps. Then, with a kind of mental shrug, decided it was pointless. It was too late to do anything about it.

Once again, time seemed to hang suspended. It must now be mid-evening; soon it would be dark. He was hungry and thirsty, but these sensations hardly seemed important.

A creak in the corridor galvanised him into alertness. Soft footsteps were approaching, the steps of someone with bare feet. They stopped outside his door, and the bolt began to move. Whoever was trying to pull it back was having difficulty. Then the door opened a few inches. A woman's voice called his name.

"Merlew!"

"Sshh!" She tiptoed into the room and closed the door behind her. "Where are you?"

"Here, in the corner." He was so glad to see her that he wanted to hug her, but was afraid of her reaction.

Merlew was peering around with distaste. "What a horrible place. Isn't there anything to sit on?"

"Some cushions."

"Oh well, they'll have to do." Her voice was restoring him to a sense of normality; there was something very down-to-earth about Merlew. She tossed a cushion against the wall and delicately lowered herself onto it.

Niall sat beside her. "Why have you come here?"

"To see what's happening to you."

"Why?"

"Because I was worried, of course!"

His heart suddenly became so light that the miseries of the past hours seemed unimportant.

"Why have they locked us up like this?"

"Sshh! Not so loud." She placed her hand on his lips; it was soft, and had a scented smell. Niall resisted the temptation to kiss it. "I can't stay long."

"Does your father know you're here?"

"No, and you must promise not to tell him." She was whispering close to his ear. The feeling of her warm breath, and of her body pressed gently against his, intoxicated him.

"Of course I wouldn't. But why has he locked us up like this?"

"It's not his fault. He has to do what they tell him. This place has been swarming with spiders all afternoon."

"What do they want?"

She whispered: "I don't know. I was hoping you could tell me."

He looked away from her, shaking his head.

After a pause, she said: "Don't you have *any* idea?"

He said: "I don't know."

Merlew placed her hands on his cheeks, and turned his face towards her. "Do you trust me?"

The question astonished him. "Of course I do!"

"And you want me to help you?"

"So long as it's not dangerous for you."

Suddenly, he knew she wanted to be kissed. It was only necessary for him to lean forward for their lips to touch. She moved one hand from his cheek to the back of his head and pressed her face tightly against his. Niall's arms went round her, and pulled her against him.

She was the first to disengage. Their position was uncomfortable, with bare shoulders pressed against the cold wall. He felt delight and incredulity as he saw that she was arranging the rest of the cushions on the floor. She apparently felt no incongruity in breaking off a kiss for this banal operation. A moment later, she had pulled him down beside her and pressed her body tightly against his.

It seemed so amazing that he found it hard to believe. Ten minutes ago, he had given up hope; now he felt he was holding everything he had ever wanted in his arms. If he had been told that he was to be executed the next morning, it would have left his delight untouched. He was aware of everything about her, of her bare legs pressed against his, of the silky material of the short tunic under his fingertips, of the breasts rising and falling against his chest, of the sweetness of her breath against his face. He kissed her ear, her neck where the hair began, her eyelids and her forehead; she stroked his hair and kissed his mouth. In the sheer pleasure of physical contact, both would have been happy to lie on the damp cushions for the rest of the night.

Somewhere below, a door slammed. She sat up and listened, then went to the door and peeped out. A moment later, she tiptoed back. Niall was sitting up again, his arm and thigh tingling as the blood flowed back into them. She sat down beside him and for another moment they kissed again. She was the first to break away.

"Listen, I'll try to find out from daddy what this is all about. But don't you have *any* idea?"

Niall said: "I killed a spider."

"You what?" She looked at him with incomprehension.

"It was on the way back from your city."

He told her the whole story: of the sandstorm, the finding of the telescopic spear, and of how he had suddenly found himself confronted by the buried death spider as it struggled out of the sand. She shuddered as he described driving the spear into its face. But when he had finished, she shook her head.

"I don't see how they could possibly know about that. They'd naturally assume it was your father."

"But they can read minds."

She shrugged impatiently. "I don't believe that. If they could read my mind, they'd have eaten me a long time ago."

"There was a spider in the next room when they brought me here. I think it was trying to read my mind."

She looked at him keenly. "What makes you think that?"

"I heard the door creak as it went out. And the boards in the corridor."

"Then what makes you think it was watching you?"

"I just had a sort of feeling . . . . You know how you feel when someone's staring at you from behind?"

"Do you often have feelings like that?"

He smiled. "Only when someone's staring at me from behind."

She sighed. "I just don't understand. Are you *sure* there's nothing else?"

"Don't you think killing a spider would explain it?"

"It might—if they knew . . ."

She suddenly stood up.

"Where are you going?"

"To talk to my father. I'm going to try and persuade him to talk to you."

"Don't tell him about the spider."

She turned and knelt on the floor beside him. "I've got to tell him. And you've got to trust him."

"But he works for them."

"Of course he does. He can't do anything else. And he's very lucky to work for them—it's better than cleaning sewers. But he doesn't like them. How could he when he saw them killing so many of our people? They even ate poor Nyris." She shuddered.

"I still don't feel it's a good idea to tell him about the spider. The less people who know, the better. I haven't even told my mother and brother."

She placed her hand round the back of his head.

"You've got to trust me. My father can't help you unless he knows the truth."

With her face so close to his, he found it impossible to object.

"All right. Do as you think best."

She leaned forward and gave him a long kiss. Then she stood up and went out. He heard the bolt slide back into place.

His happiness made it hard for him to think. Instead, he recalled over and over again every detail of the past quarter of an hour. When he remembered how much he had hated her, how often he had daydreamed of punishing her, he felt ashamed. It seemed absurd to be upset because she had called him "that skinny boy". That was simply her nature. She was a forthright person, used to giving orders and getting her own way. Yet she could be marvelously sweet and yielding. The thought of her lips pressed against his made him almost dizzy with pleasure. Her scent still lingered on his arms, and when he closed his eyes, he could imagine her lying beside him.

Suddenly, it was dark. He sat there, hugging his knees and reflecting that the smell of damp and mould would never again strike him as disagreeable; it would always remind him of Merlew. Merely to think of her name was a sensation like music.

He must have fallen asleep. A sudden light made him start in alarm; then Merlew's voice said: "Don't worry. It's only me." She was holding a small oil lamp. "You can come down now. My father wants to see you."

He followed her along the corridor. "What about my mother and Veig?"

"They're already gone. Look." She pushed open the end door; her lamp revealed an empty room.

They went down the stairs. The spider guards were no longer there. The lower floors of the building were brightly lit with the flames of many oil lamps, some of them enormous gold-coloured objects with tall glass chimneys. Merlew blew out her own lamp and pushed open a door. "In here."

It was a large room whose walls were covered with blue and gold hangings. The furniture was of the same type he had seen in Kazak's palace in Dira, but more comfortable. Half a dozen girls were seated or lying on couches; one was brushing another's hair.

Merlew clapped her hands. "Berris, Nella." Two of the girls stood up; Niall had seen them that morning, fanning King Kazak. One of them looked at him and laughed.

"What is it?"

She pointed to a metal mirror on the wall, and he saw that the left side of his face was covered with dust; so was the whole left side of his body. The other girls stared at him and began to laugh.

Merlew flushed. "That's enough. Don't waste time!"

But the girls were plainly unimpressed; one was still laughing as she laid her hand on Niall's arm and led him out of the room. He followed her along a corridor and into a large, white tiled room whose atmosphere was heavy with steam and perfume. The floor underfoot was of mosaic tiles, not unlike the ones he had seen in the temple in the desert. In the middle of the floor there was a sunken bath, circular in shape, full of blue-tinged water that steamed gently.

The girls, both of whom were olive-skinned and dark

eyed, led him to the edge of the bath; a flight of steps went down into the scented water. When one of them started to remove his tunic, Niall started nervously and tried to cling on to it. They both laughed.

"Don't be silly! You can't have a bath in your clothes!"

"But I can undress myself . . ." In the burrow, his mother and Ingeld had always undressed in the dark, and the men had averted their eyes.

The taller of the two girls shook her head. "That's our job. You don't have to be shy. We bathe the king every morning."

Niall submitted to being stripped, and the girls held his hands as he descended into the water. It was just as well; one of the top steps was slippery, and he would have lost his balance except for their firm grip.

The water was pleasantly warm, and he recognized the scent he had smelt on Merlew's hair and hands. When he was standing in the water, up to his shoulders, the girls pulled off their own tunics and jumped in beside him; the water surged up and soaked his hair. Then, while one of the girls massaged his face and torso, the other rubbed a green liquid into his hair, then rubbed it into a cloud of foamy lather.

After this, they made him sit on the steps while they poured jugs of water over him. Every time he turned his head and caught a glimpse of naked thighs, he closed his eyes. The girls noticed this and began to tease him, pulling his face against them as they washed his hair. After a few minutes of this, he decided that he looked ridiculous and joined in the laughter.

They made him stand as they dried him with enormous towels, rubbing his hair so vigorously that it made his eyes water. He was led to a couch where they rubbed oil into his body and trimmed his nails and hair. They combed his hair and brushed it, then held it in place with a narrow band of cloth round the forehead. Finally, one of them put on her tunic and went out; when she returned, she was carrying a dark blue tunic and sandals of yellow leather. When they had dressed him in these, one of them wiped the steam off a full-length mirror and showed him his reflection. He had to agree that he had never known himself so clean and so attractive. He no longer looked like a savage, but like one of the young men who had come to greet them as they approached Dira.

The door opened, and Merlew looked in. "Is he ready? Oh yes! How handsome!"

Niall blushed, but the mirror told him she was telling the truth.

"That blue colour suits you. It belonged to Corvig."

"Where is Corvig?"

"Working on the rabbit farm. They wouldn't let father keep him here." She nodded to the girls. "You can go now." As soon as the door closed behind them, she put her arms round his neck and pulled his face against hers. Then, sighing with reluctance she pushed him away.

"We mustn't keep the king waiting any longer. When you go in there, I want you to do this." She went gracefully on one knee, bowing her head. "Try it."

Niall did so, but felt awkward. "Do I have to? I've never done it before."

She placed her finger on his lip. "Do it for me. I want you to impress my father." She kissed him briefly. "I want him to like you."

"All right." If she had told him to fling himself, fully clothed, into the bath, he would have done it without hesitation.

She took his hand and led him out. The air felt cool to his

skin and he felt as if he were treading on a cushion of yielding foam.

She pushed open the door at the end of the corridor; the room inside was lit by so many lamps that it might have been daylight. The king was lounging on a heap of cushions, tended by half a dozen girls; he looked as if he had not moved since that morning.

"Ah, my dear boy. Do come in." As Niall went on one knee and averted his head, Kazak smiled with pleasure. "Well, that was done like a courtier. Excellent!" He stood up, helped by the girls, and crossed the room. "Come and sit down. You must be starving." He placed one hand lightly on Niall's shoulder.

The door clicked; Merlew had gone.

As soon as Niall was seated, a girl handed him a metal goblet and another filled it from a long-necked jug. It was the golden liquid he had drunk with Odina on the boat. Kazak watched with approval as he drained it. The drink seemed unutterably delicious, cooling his burning throat like icy nectar. Almost immediately, Niall experienced the sensation of pleasant light-headedness and the warm glow in his veins.

The girls placed carved wooden bowls of food in front of him—fruits, nuts, soft white bread and a dish containing small cooked birds, still warm from the oven. When he looked questioningly at Kazak, the king said: "That is all for you. I have eaten already." He gestured to one of the girls. "Krista, play our guest some music to aid his digestion."

She took up a stringed instrument, sat on the floor in front of them and began to sing in a sweet, clear voice. Kazak lay back on his cushions and closed his eyes in an expression of contentment. Niall was too ravenous to pay attention to the music. Yet in spite of his hunger, he ate sparingly. He knew that too much food would make him sleepy, and some intuition told him that he should keep his wits about him. For the same reason, he resisted the temptation to drain the second cup of the honey-coloured liquid, and sipped it slowly.

When he had finished eating, one of the girls came forward with a damp, scented cloth and wiped his hands and mouth; another dried him with a soft towel.

The girl ceased playing. Kazak seemed to wake up. He looked at Niall with a benevolent smile.

"Had enough?"

"Yes thank you, sire."

"Good. Then we can talk." He turned to the girls and clapped his hands. They gathered the food bowls and went out.

Kazak rearranged his cushions closer to Niall and sat on them with his legs crossed. He said:

"Well, young man, you seem to be causing us quite an amount of trouble."

Niall blushed. "I'm very sorry. But I don't know why."

Kazak looked Niall direct in the eyes. "Don't you?"

Niall answered truthfully. "No."

Kazak frowned, staring down at his feet; the movement accentuated his double chins. He said finally:

"You killed a spider."

Niall had to prevent his voice from trembling as he answered: "Yes."

Kazak stared at him. "How?"

"With a kind of spear . . ."

"This?" From under a cushion, Kazak produced the metal cylinder.

"Yes."

The king held it out to him. "Show me how it works."

Niall took it from him, located the concentric circle in the metal, and pressed it; the rod slid open. Kazak watched carefully. Niall pressed again; the rod contracted. Kazak held out his hand, and Niall gave it to him. Kazak located the circle, and pressed it with his thumb. Nothing happened. He pressed again and again. Finally he handed it back to Niall.

"Is there some trick?"

"I don't think so." Niall pressed, and the rod expanded. Kazak took it from him and tried again. Nothing happened. After trying for perhaps a minute, Kazak dropped it on the floor with a motion of irritation.

"Why do you think you can do it and I can't."

"I don't know." It had never occurred to him for a moment that the mechanism would not work for other people.

"Tell me the story of how you found it."

Obediently, Niall repeated the story of the sandstorm, of the ruined city, and of the glittering machine. Kazak reached behind him and found a bleached board and a piece of charcoal.

"Could you draw it for me?"

Niall made a crude sketch of the machine, realising, as he did so, that he had forgotten many details. Kazak stared at it for a long time. He asked:

"Can the rest of your family open and close the rod?"

"I don't know."

"Why not?"

"I . . . didn't show it to them."

Kazak nodded sympathetically. "Afraid your brother might want to take it from you?"

"Yes."

"All right. Tell me about killing the spider."

Niall repeated the story as he had told it to Merlew. Kazak interrupted to ask:

"Were you looking into its face?"

"Yes."

"Yet you were still able to kill it?"

"Yes."

Kazak said: "It is almost impossible for a human being to kill a spider, unless he can take it unaware. They can knock a man down by sheer force of will. Why do you think you were able to kill this one?"

"Perhaps it was dazed from being buried in the sand."

Kazak shook his head. "No. It still had time to send an alarm signal before it died. Did it not try to resist you?"

"Yes."

"With its will-power?"

"Yes."

"Then how were you able to kill it?"

"I don't know." To Niall, the question seemed absurd. It had all happened in the blink of an eyelid, and he had not even thought about it.

Kazak refilled his goblet from the jug and sipped it thoughtfully. He looked at Niall from underneath his bristling eyebrows. "Do you begin to understand why the spiders are so interested in you?"

Niall said: "Because I killed a spider?"

"Not because you killed a spider. Because you were *able* to kill a spider."

Niall shook his head. Kazak said patiently:

"I will explain. When the body of the dead spider was found, they discovered that it had been pierced through the brain. It had died instantly. Yet it had had time to send out an alarm signal. That meant that its will was fully awake and active. It should have been impossible for you even to raise that spear." He was staring into Niall's face, watching for some reaction, but Niall could only nod uncomprehendingly. Kazak went on:

"It was the first time in more than two hundred years that a spider had been killed by some other creature. The murder—because that is how they regarded it—caused a sort of panic. It meant that spiders were no longer invulnerable. They felt they had to find the killer at all costs. That is why they invaded the land of Dira. That is why more than fifty of my people died."

Niall said: "I'm sorry."

Kazak sighed. "Regrets are futile. That is also why your father died. It didn't take them long to find out that you and he were near the fortress at the time." He avoided Niall's eyes as he said this. "Now do you begin to understand why they were so anxious to find you?"

Niall averted his eyes. "To kill me?"

He was astonished when Kazak said: "No. Not necessarily to kill *you*. They think your father killed the spider."

After a long pause, Niall asked: "What then?"

Kazak said: "If you were the only one, it would make sense to kill you. You see, when things like this happen, they often happen to many people at the same time. I don't understand why. It seems to be a law of nature. If they kill you, there may still be dozens—perhaps hundreds—more like you." He stared into Niall's eyes. "But while you are alive, you can be of use to them."

Niall shook his head. "How?"

"Do you think you could recognise others like you?"

Even if Kazak's eyes had not been boring into his own, Niall would have recognised that everything depended on this question. Kazak was asking him to admit that he was different from others, and that he knew he was different. It was a moment when each knew precisely what was in the other's mind. Niall said finally:

"I think so."

Kazak's face relaxed into a smile. He leaned forward and

slapped Niall on the shoulder. "That's what I wanted to hear." Niall could sense his relief, and it surprised him; there had been no moment when Kazak had not seemed master of the situation.

Kazak moved off the cushions, stretched his legs, then relaxed once more against the wall. "Good, now we can discuss this sensibly." He refilled his goblet and handed the jug to Niall, who refilled his own goblet but took only a small sip. "But first, let us be quite clear about one thing. Would you be willing to work for the spiders?"

"Work for them?" Niall gaped with astonishment.

Kazak said with a touch of impatience: "Help them locate others like you?"

"But how could I?"

Kazak smiled. "It's perfectly simple. The spiders will comb the deserts for savages. In fact, they already know where most of them are located."

"They know?"

"Of course. Why do you think they send out those damn balloons all the time?"

Niall said: "But in that case . . ." He stopped, too bewildered to go on.

"In that case, why don't they capture them all at once? Because they *need* the free human beings—the savages, as they call them."

Niall was puzzled. "In what way?"

"For breeding." He smiled benevolently at Niall. "That's what most of my people are going to be used for. Haven't you noticed what's wrong with most of the people in this city?" Niall waited. "They're stupid. Most of them are little better than morons. That's because the spiders deliberately breed them for stupidity. If a child seems more intelligent or more enterprising than the others they kill him."

Niall felt his brain was spinning. "But why?"

"Why? Because intelligent human beings are a threat. To begin with, they don't like being eaten. In the days when human beings were masters of this planet, they used to breed cattle for food. Now the spiders breed people for the same purpose."

Niall said: "But only the slaves."

Kazak smiled at him pityingly. "Only the slaves! And what do you suppose happens to the others?"

"They work for the spiders."

"And when they've finished working?"

Already sensing the answer, Niall said: "They are sent to the great happy place."

Kazak laughed brutally. "The slaughterhouse."

Niall shook his head. "You mean they're *all* going to be eaten—all the servants, all the commanders?" He was thinking of Odina.

Kazak nodded. "That's right. Everybody who's not in the secret." He added reflectively. "I don't think they'll bother to eat me—I'm too tough. Or Merlew."

"Is Merlew in the secret?"

"Of course."

Niall felt chilled and shocked. It was hard to think of Merlew as an accomplice in this mass deception and murder.

Kazak seemed to read his thoughts. "You have to look at this sensibly. The spiders are the masters. They can do what they like, whether we agree or not. And although you might not believe this, they're not really as bad as you might suppose. Some of them are quite remarkable people. You should think of them as people, by the way, not insects. They can sense our feelings about them, and don't like being regarded as insects. So get into the habit of thinking of them as people. And they *are* the masters. They can do what they like. It doesn't bother you to eat a dead bird, does it? Well, it doesn't bother them to eat a dead human. To them, we're only intelligent cattle. Yet I've known people who kept birds as pets—they loved them as much as their own children. The spiders feel the same about human beings. They often get quite fond of us. Now if its a choice between being eaten and being regarded as a pet, I know exactly where I stand. I prefer to stay alive."

Niall was as much impressed by the king's flow of words as by his reasoning; it was the first time in his life he had heard anyone speak so fluently. Kazak's fine, masculine voice had an amazing range of tones, from caressing intimacy to passionate assertion. Niall found he was listening to it like music, yet at no point did he feel that Kazak was using it simply for effect.

He had to collect his thoughts to ask the question that was troubling him. "If the spiders kill the intelligent children, why do they need the desert people for breeding? We are more intelligent than most of these servants of the spiders."

"A good question." Kazak was like an approving schoolmaster, and Niall experienced a flash of pride. "The spiders spend ten generations reducing their servants to stupidity, and then find their servants turning into imbeciles. Where do you think the slaves come from? They're the tenth generation of people deliberately bred for stupidity. That's why they need new breeding stock—like yourself."

"Like me?" Niall was taken by surprise.

"Of course. Your job will be to father children."

Niall felt himself blushing. "And the women . . . how do they feel about it?"

Kazak said gravely: "They have no objection whatever. Except, of course, frustration at being segregated."

Niall suddenly recalled the snub-nosed girl who had lured him into the bushes; for the first time, he understood what had been happening. The thought made his brain whirl.

Kazak said: "So I think you can begin to see why I chose to cooperate with the spider people. It was not simply a question of my own survival. It was a desire to do the best I can for my people. Of course, the men aren't so badly off. But I don't want to see the women turned into breeding machines—particularly my own daughter. She seems to be rather fond of you, by the way." Niall felt himself flushing with pleasure and avoided Kazak's eyes. "Then, of course, there's your own mother. How would you like to see her penned up in the women's quarters, producing a stranger's baby once a year? Upsetting? You have the power to make sure it doesn't happen."

He drained his goblet and slowly refilled it, giving Niall time to reflect. Niall stared past the king's head, through the window; the full moon was rising in the black night sky.

"Are you sure the spiders . . . the spider people want me to work for them?" he asked finally.

Kazak nodded. "Quite sure."

"When I came in this afternoon, I felt they all wanted to kill me."

"Of course. Because for them you represent a danger. If they were certain—" he emphasised the word—"that you were an ally, they'd soon feel different."

Niall looked at him with polite disbelief. "You think they would?"

"Of course. They need your help."

"But I killed one of their kind."

"They don't know that, and I shan't tell them."

"Won't they guess?"

"Not if you don't allow them to. As far as they're concerned, the man who killed the spider is now dead—your unfortunate father. I was very sorry about that, by the way; I liked him. But we have to look at things practically. You killed a spider, they killed your father. Now you're even, and it's time to forget your grudges and work together."

"What shall I have to do?"

"We'll discuss that tomorrow. Then I shall take you to see the Spider Lord." Niall went pale. "There's nothing to fear. I think you'll find the interview pleasant enough. I shall do most of the talking."

"May I ask you one more question?"

"As many as you like, my dear boy."

"How can you be certain they're not deceiving *you*?"

Kazak smiled imperturbably. "You mean how can I be certain they won't kill me when I've ceased to be useful? Simple logic. They need me. They need someone to organise all the human beings in this city, someone they can trust. *That's* the point I'm making, Niall." It was the first time he had called Niall by his name. "They need people they can trust. Why should they eat you or me? They've thousands—hundreds of thousands—of people they can eat whenever they want to. But they've almost no intelligent human beings they can trust. That's what they really need. Besides, they're not savages, you know. They're highly civilised creatures. They have their thinkers and their artists and their statesmen—I've been talking with their leading statesman all afternoon, a spider called Dravig. You'd be amazed how fascinating these people are, once you get to know them." He studied Niall's expression and recognised the shade of doubt. "I know what you're thinking—that it's hard to feel friendly towards people who are eating human beings. I feel the same. But if they trust you, they don't mind you protecting those close to you. They accept that as normal and natural."

"What about my mother and brother? Will you let them into the secret?"

Kazak frowned thoughtfully. "I don't know. Not yet, at

any rate. I have to make up my mind that they can be trusted. You see, if they can't be trusted, and we let them into the secret, we're simply endangering their lives. I haven't even let my own sons into the secret. It's better for them not to know it." He looked into Niall's eyes. "And of course, I don't have to emphasise to you how important it is to keep all this to yourself. The spider people are ruthless with those who betray their trust."

Niall nodded. "I know."

"Good." Kazak leaned forward and patted his shoulder. "I think you and I are going to make a good partnership." He clapped his hands. "Now, do you feel like more music?"

The girls came in. Without being bidden, the lute player took up her instrument and began to sing. The other girls joined in softly. Their singing was incredibly skillful and beautiful. But Niall found it difficult to concentrate. The thought of the secret filled him with a mixture of excitement and anxiety. He already knew that Veig would refuse to cooperate. Veig's nature was too straight-forward; he would never feel anything but loathing for the spiders. As to his mother, how could she forgive the killers of her husband? If he now refused to cooperate with Kazak, he was condemning them to death . . .

Kazak touched him on the shoulder. "I'm afraid you're falling asleep." It was true that he had difficulty keeping his eyes open. "Would you like to go to your sleeping chamber?" Niall nodded gratefully. "Mirris, show him to his room—the one opposite Merlew's . . ." He smiled at Niall. "Sleep as long as you like. You have a long day tomorrow. Don't forget this." He tossed Niall the metal cylinder.

Mirris was one of the two girls who had bathed him. She gave him a mischievous backward glance as she led him up the stairs. "The king seems fond of you."

"Is he?"

"You ought to know!" She led him along a corridor whose carpet deadened their footsteps and flung open a door. He followed her into a bedroom that was so luxurious that for a moment he thought there must be some mistake.

"Are you sure this is mine?"

"Quite sure."

The bed was at least two feet above the floor and covered with a gold-coloured cloth. Underfoot, the carpet felt as soft as young grass. The lights burned in tiny crystal vases, emitting a rosy glimmer.

She pulled back the coverlets. "Those are your night clothes." She pointed to a blue garment that hung over the end of the couch. "Shall I help you to undress?"

For a moment he thought she was joking; when he saw her eyes were serious, he smiled. "No, I think I can do it alone."

She gazed up at him and he could feel the radiated warmth of her body.

"But now you live in the palace, you don't have to do things alone. We are here to do things for you. I could be your personal servant. Would you like that?"

"I'm sure the king would object."

"Oh no, I'm sure he wouldn't. Would you like me to ask him?"

It was then, quite suddenly, that Niall found himself aware of her thoughts. It seemed to happen because he was looking down into her eyes, and there was some natural sympathy between their minds. All at once, he knew that she was offering herself because the king had ordered her to. He also knew that she was delighted to obey— that there was nothing she wanted more than to be his servant. He only had to say the word, and she would regard herself as his property, to do with as he liked.

Then the thought of Merlew crossed his mind. He shook his head. "I don't think that would be a good idea."

Her face clouded with disappointment. "Why not? You need a servant."

"The princess might not agree."

Her face became puzzled. "Why not? I am only a servant. She would have no cause to be jealous."

What Niall glimpsed in her mind perplexed and disturbed him. It was almost as if they were talking about two different Merlews. He was suddenly chilled by a sense of foreboding, of learning something he would prefer not to know.

He forced himself to smile at her. "Let me ask her first."

"All right." Her face became radiant again. "Can I get you something before you go to bed—a drink, something to eat?"

He shook his head. "No thank you."

She dropped him a curtsy before she went out, and he realised that she already regarded herself as his servant.

He sat down on the edge of the bed, which yielded softly beneath his weight, and stared blankly at his reflection in the mirror on the wall. It was like looking at a stranger. Yet it was not merely his physical appearance—the blue uniform of a king's son, the white braid round the hair—that brought this sense of estrangement. It was the feeling that all his inner certainties had been undermined.

Two hours ago, he had been in a daze of happiness to realise that Merlew found him attractive. It seemed impossible that she could love him; but when she kissed him in the bathroom, he had come to feel that it was incredible but true.

Now that certainty had evaporated. It had happened as the servant girl stared up into his face. Suddenly, he had realised that she was a bribe. Like this bedroom, she was intended to keep him happy. But she had not told him the truth—that Kazak had ordered her to be his servant. She had made it sound as if it was her own idea, and that she would have to ask the king for permission. He had to be flattered into cooperation.

Had Merlew also been ordered to bribe him—with kisses, with implied promises of love? Now, suddenly, he seemed to hear her voice: "What, that skinny boy? You must be joking," and his heart seemed to wither inside him.

The uncertainty was intolerable. He slipped off his sandals and crossed the room. His door opened noiselessly. Facing him across the corridor was a door painted royal green; the handle was shaped like a serpent. As he reached out for it, he hoped for a moment that he would find the door locked; yet even before he touched it, he knew it would be open. The handle yielded, and he pushed the door ajar.

The room was lit with the same rose-coloured flames as his own. At a dressing table on the other side of the bed, Merlew was sitting, brushing her hair before the mirror. She was dressed in a long, silky garment of a creamy white colour and her feet were bare. Her yellow hair was spread over her shoulders, and she was completely absorbed. If she had moved her eyes a fraction of an inch, she would have seen Niall's face watching her through the open door; but she was gazing into her own eyes, lost in thought.

He opened his mouth to speak to her, then changed his mind. Her beauty seemed to hurt his senses; he was unwilling to expose himself to further misery. Then, as he watched her face, his mind seemed to find her thought-vibration. For a moment, he was quite certain that she would sense his presence and turn round. But her absorption made her oblivious.

Then, quite suddenly, he was inside her body, drifting along with the stream of her feelings and sensations. In that moment, all his misery and jealousy disappeared; since his own identity was merged in hers, jealousy would have been an absurdity. He was aware of her essence, her reality. A few moments before, she had been an imaginary girl, a dream image created by his desire and inexperience. Now, suddenly, she was a real person, and he was ashamed of his stupidity. The girl he was now looking at was the Merlew he had glimpsed through the mind of the servant girl, who had known her since childhood. This reality was at once more complex and more commonplace than his dream image of femininity.

The real Merlew was generous, good natured and easy to please. She was also imperious and capricious; she regarded having her own way as a law of nature.

At this moment, she was wondering idly what had happened to Niall. She liked Niall. The skinny boy, whom she had found interesting but slightly ridiculous, had improved greatly in the months since she had last seen him. He was taller and stronger, and some experience had made him more mature. Although she had been carrying out her father's orders, it had been a pleasure to make Niall fall in love with her. He was a good-looking young man, and she liked good-looking young men. At home she had been surrounded by them; here in the spider city, she felt deprived. Of course, Niall was shy and awkward, with no experience of love-making; but she could soon remedy that. In fact, she was looking forward to becoming his teacher; it gave her pleasure to teach men the rudiments of love-making . . .

Niall closed the door silently and went back to his own room. He felt like laughing aloud. It seemed incredible that so much misery and jealousy could evaporate so quickly and so completely. He still found Merlew beautiful and desirable, but the feeling was unadulterated with illusions;

he felt as though he had been married to her for ten years. He also felt as though he had aged ten years. It was not an unpleasant sensation.

All desire to sleep had vanished. He went to the window and looked out; the main avenue outside was bathed in moonlight. It looked totally deserted. By standing at an angle, he could see the white tower; it seemed to be shining in the moonlight with a milky glow. At the same time, he experienced an inexpressible sense of longing which was somehow amplified by his new feeling of freedom. Like the moon, the tower seemed remote and untouchable. Now he no longer dreamed of Merlew, the tower seemed to have become the focus of his deepest desire.

He picked up the metal cylinder from the chair where he had dropped it, and touched the button that made it expand, observing as he did so that it was not necessary to exert any pressure. The end of the rod caused a tingling in his fingers; it was the same sensation that he had experienced that morning, pressing his hands against the tower.

He went out into the corridor and closed the door behind him. At the far end, someone went past, mounting the stairs; it was one of the servant girls. He stood until she was gone, then went to the head of the stairs. As he began to descend, he heard the sound of a door closing softly. Merlew was standing in the corridor. As he watched, she knocked gently on his own door, then turned the handle and entered. Niall went on down the stairs.

The hallway was empty. He tried the main door; it was locked. But the door into the rear courtyard was open. So was the gateway into the street. Niall made no attempt at concealment; he was aware that the spiders hunted by will, not by sight, and his strange inner-calm gave him a sense of invulnerability.

The sight of the tower at the end of the avenue released

a sense of serene exultancy. Even among these towering buildings, it looked enormous, and the moonlight seemed to magnify its size. His eyes remained fixed on it as he walked along the avenue. When he reached the square, he observed two wolf-spider guards standing outside the entrance of the building with the black façade. They watched him without curiosity as he crossed the square; anyone who walked so casually in the moonlight must have an official reason for being abroad.

Near the tower, the smell of explosive still lingered in the air. The earth underfoot was soft where the crater had been filled in.

Niall walked slowly round the foot of the tower, staring at its milky surface. At close quarters, the glow seemed stronger than the moonlight, as if it came from inside. And as he stared at it, a curious sense of anticipation swept through his body. The rod in his hand was now tingling, prickling against the damp skin as if emitting tiny points of light. It was the sensation he had experienced in the past when dowsing for water, and it seemed to draw him towards a particular spot on the northern side of the tower. As he approached, the sense of inner certainty became stronger. He took the ends of the rod in both hands, and as soon as he did so, experienced a dizzying sensation that made him feel the ground was swaying. He looked up, and the tower seemed immense, stretching up as far as the eye could see. The metal contacted its surface, and the dizziness became a sudden acute nausea; for a moment, he was choking. His knees were buckling, and he was staggering forward into a whirlpool of darkness. Then his senses cleared, and the darkness changed into light. He was standing inside the tower.

THIS IMPRESSION lasted only as long as it took his eyes to refocus. Then, with a shock that made him feel breathless, he found himself standing on a beach. For a moment, he felt he was dreaming. But there could be no doubting the reality of the waves breaking a few yards from his feet, or of the slimy, weed-covered rocks that stretched into the sea.

Niall had no doubt what had happened. His grandfather had told him too many tales of magic for him not to recognise an example of the enchanter's art. He stared up at the pale blue sky overhead, at the immense line of cliffs that extended into the distance, and sought some clue to his present situation. The coolness of the breeze, and the presence of drifting white clouds in the sky, argued that he was far from the desert. The trees on the clifftop were unlike any he had ever seen; they were taller, and of a darker green. The sea itself looked more grey and cold than the sea he had crossed two days ago.

It was when he was looking along the beach for the

second time that he saw the old man sitting on a rock. The sight made him start; he was certain the beach had been empty a few moments ago. Now he had no doubt that he was in the presence of the magician.

When the old man raised his head, Niall received another shock; it was his grandfather Jomar. It was only as he approached closer that he began to experience doubts. This man was taller, and there was a completely different quality about his gaze. Yet the resemblance was remarkable; he might have been Jomar's brother.

As Niall came closer, the man stood up. His garments struck Niall as completely outlandish. They were of a uniform shade of pale grey, and covered his entire body from his neck to his feet. The trouserlegs terminated in polished black shoes.

Niall raised his hand, palm outward, in the desert salute. Because the man was older, it would have been impolite to speak first.

The old man smiled; his eyes were of a pale blue. "Your name is Niall." It was a statement, not a question.

"Yes, sire."

"You needn't call me sire. My name is Steeg. At least, that's what you'd better call me. How do you do?" But when Niall reached out to clasp arms, he drew back. "I don't think you'd better try to touch me." His smile made it plain this was not a rebuke. He pointed to a rock. "Would you like to sit down?"

Niall sat on the weed-covered boulder; the old man re-seated himself on his rock. He looked at Niall for several moments without speaking, then asked:

"Do you know where you are?"

"Inside . . . I was inside the white tower."

"You *are* inside the white tower. Close your eyes." Niall obeyed. "Now feel the rock you are sitting on." Niall did so, and was astonished to realise that it had a smooth, flat surface. He opened his eyes and looked down at the green weed and the sea-worn granite. When he touched it, he could see that it was an illusion; his fingertips encountered something more like smooth wood.

The old man said: "Take off your shoes and feel the sand." Niall did so, and found that his feet were now resting on a hard, flat surface. When walking across it, it had never occurred to him to doubt that it was sand because it looked like sand.

Niall said: "You must be a great magician."

The man shook his head. "I am not any kind of a magician." He pointed to the beach. "And this is not a magical illusion. It is what used to be called a panoramic hologram. When men were still on earth, they used to be the main attraction of children's amusement parks."

Niall asked eagerly: "Do you know about the time when men were lords of the earth?"

"I know everything about it."

"And are you one of those ancient men?"

The old man shook his head. "No, in fact, I am not really here at all, as you'll see if you try to touch me." He held out his hand; when Niall tried to touch it, his fingers passed through it. He felt totally unalarmed. The old man's smile was so pleasant, and his manner so casual and intimate, that it was obvious there was no cause for fear.

"But you must be very old."

"No. I am far younger than you. In fact, I am only a few minutes old." He smiled at Niall's bewilderment. "Don't worry. Everything will be explained in due course. But before we begin, I think we'd better move upstairs."

Niall glanced in bewilderment at the sky. As he did so, it vanished, and he found himself looking at a white, luminous ceiling. In place of the cliffs and the distant horizons there were the curved white walls of the tower. He was not seated on a weed-covered rock, but on a kind of solid stool made of pale wood; the old man sat on an identical stool. This circular room otherwise seemed to be empty, except for a central column stretching from floor to ceiling. But its surface seemed somehow unstable, as if it were in continuous slow motion, like smoke.

The old man stood up. "Would you like to follow me?" He walked towards the column and vanished into it, disappearing completely. But his voice issued from the smoky white surface. "Step into it, as I did."

When Niall obeyed, he found himself surrounded by a kind of white fog. Then he was floating upwards. A moment later, he stopped with a slight jerk.

"Step forward again," the old man said.

For a moment, Niall thought he was under the night sky. He could see the moon and stars overhead; the spider city lay around them. A few hundred yards away, he could see the black-fronted building of the Spider Lord. He could even see the wolf spiders standing on guard before its door. But when he stepped forward, his outstretched hand encountered glass. It was so transparent that it reflected none of the light that filled the room.

He pointed to the spider guards. "But can't they see us?"

"No. The light can enter the walls but cannot leave again."

This room was comfortably furnished with furniture not unlike that of Kazak's palace. The chairs and the couch were covered with a black substance like leather. There was a soft black carpet on the floor. The only unusual item was a device like a tall black box which stood against the glass wall; on its sloping upper surface was a panel of opaque white glass. A row of control buttons underneath it reminded Niall of the strange machine in the desert.

"What is that?" he asked.

"That is the most valuable object in this place. It cost more than this whole city to make."

"But what does it do?"

"To begin with, it creates me."

Niall recalled the creation myths his mother had told him as a child. "Is it a god?" he asked with awe.

"Oh no, just a machine."

"But I thought only a god could create."

"That is untrue. You see, you are also creating me."

That sounded so absurd that Niall could only stare. The old man said:

"I am reacting to your questions and your responses. Even my appearance is borrowed from your memory."

It took Niall some time to absorb this.

"And this tower?"

"This tower was created by men before they left the earth. It was intended to be a museum—a place in which the history of the earth would be stored. When it was almost completed, men realised that the earth would pass through the tail of an immense radioactive comet."

"What is a comet?"

"I will show you. Look."

As he spoke, the sky overhead changed. The full moon became a crescent, hanging above the rooftops. The buildings of the city were suddenly transformed; their windows filled with lights, and searchlight beams illuminated the façades of the buildings in the square. And in the southern sky, directly above the great avenue, there hung a dazzling trail of white vapour, terminating at its lower end in a mass of blue-green light. It looked like a giant version of the falling stars Niall had seen so often in the desert except that instead of moving, it hung motionless.

"This is the comet Opik," the old man said. "It's head is

twelve thousand miles in diameter, and the coma—the shell surrounding the nucleus—is fifty thousand miles across. The tail is more than seven million miles long.

"It is not as frightening as it looks. This head is fully of tiny particles, most of them not much bigger than a grain of sand. Even if it had struck the earth directly, it would not have destroyed it. But Opik came from somewhere beyond the solar system, and was powerfully radioactive—that means it contained substances that would destroy most animals. Men had less than a year to prepare to evacuate the earth. More than a hundred million people—most of the earth's population—escaped in giant space transporters. But before leaving, they completed this tower, for the days when men would return."

Niall shook his head. "I don't understand."

"That is why they built this tower— so the men of the future would understand."

Niall said sadly: "I am afraid I am too stupid."

"That is untrue. Your intelligence is equal to that of the man who built this machine—Torwald Steeg. But Steeg died a long time ago, and you find his language difficult to understand."

"But you said your name was Steeg."

The old man smiled. "I have a right to the name. I am all that remains of Steeg's mind." He pointed to the black box. "You see, I am not really here. I am inside that computer. And you are not really speaking to me—you are speaking to that computer."

"What is a . . . computer?"

"All your questions will be answered. But it will take a long time. Are you willing to stay here until you are satisfied?"

"Yes . . . of course. But . . ."

"But you are worried about your mother and brother."

Niall experienced a flash of superstitious fear; it was unnerving to feel that not even his thoughts were private.

"How did you know?"

"I became aware of you—or rather, the Steegmaster became aware of you— " he pointed to the computer—"when you activated the flying machine in the desert. Ever since then, we have been observing you. It was the Steegmaster that summoned you here tonight."

"Why?"

"That question will also be answered. But first, there are many other things you must know. Are you ready to begin now? Or would you prefer to sleep?"

"I don't feel like sleep. And besides . . ."

"You are worried about your mother and brother."

"Yes. I am afraid of what Kazak will do to them when he finds I am gone."

"He will do nothing to them. He will not dare to tell the Spider Lord that he allowed you to walk out. So he will pretend that he is keeping you under observation in his palace. And he will treat your mother and brother like honoured guests, because he knows that as long as he holds them in his palace, you will want to return."

"How do you know this? Can you read his mind?"

"No, not as you can. But we have also been observing Kazak for a long time. We can predict how he will react. For all his cunning, he is not a difficult man to understand."

"And the Spider Lord? Can you understand his mind?"

"Very easily. You see, he has only one desire—to remain master of the earth. At the moment, his chief desire is to persuade you to help him."

"Why?"

"Because he is afraid there are others of your kind. He wants to find them all, to destroy them. When he has done that, he will destroy you and all your family."

This was something that Niall had suspected; but to hear it expressed so bluntly made his heart sink.

"Can he be defeated?" he asked.

"If he could not be defeated, he would not be afraid of you."

He asked quickly: "How can it be done?"

The old man shook his head. "You are trying to learn too fast. We must begin at the beginning. Come with me."

As he passed Niall, his clothing brushed Niall's bare arm, but Niall felt nothing; yet he observed that the garments made rustling noises, and that his footfalls were audible on the carpet.

He followed the old man into the column, and was again surrounded by white mist. His body sank gently, as if it had become a feather.

As soon as he stepped into the room, he knew it was one of Steeg's magical illusions; it was far too large to be accommodated in the tower. It was a broad gallery, about a hundred feet long, whose walls were covered with a rich brocade of blue and gold and with many pictures. At regular intervals there were pedestals with busts and statues. Crystal chandeliers hung from the decorated ceiling.

Through the windows, Niall caught glimpses of an unknown city. It was smaller than the spider city—hardly more than a small town—and the houses were only two or three storeys high. It was divided by a river—the tower stood on its bank—crossed by several bridges of arched stone, and seemed to be surrounded by a wall with square towers at regular intervals. Beyond the city there were green hills with terraces. People in bright coloured clothes were going about their business through the streets and squares.

Niall was fascinated by the pictures on the walls. It was the first time he had ever seen a painting, and he was astounded that human faces could be rendered with such accuracy. He found the art of perspective even more incredible. He could see clearly that he was looking at a flat surface, yet streets and landscapes looked as if they were part of a view from a window.

"Where are we?"

"In a city that no longer exists. It was called Florence, and it was once the intellectual centre of the western world."

Niall shook his head. "I cannot understand your words. What is an intellectual centre? And what is the western world?"

"You will soon understand all these things. But first, your mind has to be prepared to receive the knowledge. I want you to lie down here."

In the centre of the gallery there was a machine of blue coloured metal; its lower part consisted of a bed or couch above which was suspended a metal canopy whose lower face was covered by opaque glass.

"What is it for?"

"We call it the peace machine. Its purpose is to remove all tensions from the body and mind. After that, you will be ready to begin the process of absorption."

"Absorption?"

"The real name for learning. What you learn is absorbed by your mind as food is absorbed by the body, and becomes a part of you."

The surface of the bed was so soft that Niall sank into it as if it had been made of eiderdown. As soon as he did so, a light came on behind the glass above him and there was a faint humming sound. He immediately experienced a sense of relaxation so deep that it was almost painful. Aches and tensions of which he had not even been aware now became apparent as they were in the process of dissolving away. His head throbbed as a slight headache intensified for a moment, then vanished. It was as if gentle, unseen fingers were penetrating his body and untying knots of frustration. As he sighed deeply, he felt as if he was expelling all the miseries of a lifetime. The peace was like the total security of a baby falling asleep at the breast. Images floated lazily through his brain, like voices from another world. With no attempt to resist, he sank into the warm depths of unconsciousness.

As awareness returned, there were brief memories of dreams and strange events which vanished as he opened his eyes. For a moment, he struggled to remember where he was; it was as if he was awakening from one dream to another. The real world seemed strangely simple and obvious when compared with the complexity of the world of dreams.

He turned his head sideways and found himself looking at the bust of a full-bearded man with a strange nose and firm mouth. The inscription underneath it said: Plato. It took him a moment to realise that he was able to read the word carved into the pedestal. Then he sat up in excitement. He was alone in the gallery; the sun streamed in through the windows. He struggled off the bed and stood in front of the bust. Underneath the inscription there was a printed notice under glass. With a delight that made him feel drunk, he read it aloud: "Plato—real name Aristocles—was born in Athens in 427 B.C. His nickname, Plato, means the Broad, and referred to his broad shoulders. Frustrated in his political ambitions, Plato founded the Academy, perhaps the first university . . ." What amazed Niall was that he understood the meaning of the words. He knew that Athens was a city in ancient Greece, that political ambitions meant an attempt to become a statesman, that a university was a school for advanced learning. When he looked out of the window, he knew that he was looking at a town that rose to prominence in mediaeval Italy, that the river was called the Arno, that the tall white building with the red dome was the cathedral, the square, dark building nearby the old palace of the Medicis, in front of which Savonarola had been burned . . .

He sat down on a chair near the window and stared down at the river. It was difficult to know precisely how much he knew, for he had to formulate a mental question before he knew whether he knew the answer. It was as if he had inherited somebody else's library, and was not sure exactly what books it contained.

The old man stepped out of the white column. "Good morning. Did you sleep well?"

"I think so."

"Are you hungry?"

"Yes." He had been so excited that he had failed to notice it.

"Then before we do anything else, you had better eat. Follow me."

He led Niall to a small room containing a few tables and chairs; out of the window, there was a view of the far side of the river with its grey city wall. Next to the window an oblong metal box stood against the wall; the surface was of a dull silver colour. "This is the food synthesiser. I am afraid we have no fresh food here. But the art of synthesis had reached a remarkable stage of perfection in the last days before men left the planet. You choose what you want by pressing the button, and it will be delivered at the hatch below."

Facing Niall on the wall by the side of the machine was a chart with a list of food and drink: fillet steak, ham and eggs, roast turkey, nut cutlet, apple pie with cream, pecan pie, cheesecake, ice cream . . . By the side of each item was a picture and a silver button.

The old man said: "If I were you, I should stick to items you can eat with your fingers. The grilled lamb chops are usually excellent. So is the roast duck. And I believe the tomato soup is of unusual quality."

When Niall pressed the buttons he had selected, there was a whirring noise inside the metal box. Two minutes later, a small door opened with a click and three plates and a cup slid out on a metal tray. Niall carried it to the table near the window. One of its frames stood open, and a pleasant breeze blew in. From outside he could hear various sounds: the shouts of boatmen on the river, the splash of oars in the water, the clopping of horses' hooves and the creaking of carts.

He was surprised when the old man drew back a chair and sat down opposite him.

"How can you do that if your body isn't solid?"

"This is completely controlled environment. The Steegmaster can do almost anything." He waved his hand and all the chairs in the room began to move in and out under the tables; then the tables floated off the floor and performed a waltz in mid-air before settling down again. Accustomed to wonders, Niall merely smiled.

The food was excellent; Niall had never tasted such flavours; the tomato soup was rich and creamy, with just the right degree of astringency; the lamb cutlets, with rings of paper around the bone, were lightly browned outside and pink and delicate inside; the cherry flavoured cheesecake was of such superlative quality that he was tempted to have a second helping; the pistachio and walnut ice cream struck him as the most amazing food he had ever tasted. Even so, it cost him an effort to swallow the final mouthful. Totally replete, feeling that his stomach was on the point of protest, he sat back in the chair, wiping his sticky fingers on a damp cloth supplied in a sealed packet.

"Men who could eat such food every day must have lived the life of gods."

"An interesting observation. But the life of gods consisted in appreciation of being godlike, and the men who created the food synthesiser were totally preoccupied with trivial problems. They were no more godlike than King Kazak or your own father."

What delighted Niall was that he could understand everything the old man said; a few hours earlier, such a sentence would have been beyond his comprehension. He asked:

"How did you teach me to read?"

"A simple technique known as sleep learning. The knowledge was implanted directly in the memory cells of your brain."

"Why did you not teach me about the men who made the synthesiser at the same time?"

"In that case, you would lose all the pleasure of learning for yourself. And the pleasure is the most important part of learning."

Now he was becoming accustomed to the old man, Niall was beginning to observe that his responses were not as natural and spontaneous as those of a human being. It was not something he would have noticed if he had not been aware that Steeg was a man-made illusion; he would have assumed simply that age had destroyed some of his spontaneity. But now he was beginning to see that Steeg's range of human responses was limited. He smiled at the right moments, he nodded in response to Niall's comments, he moistened his lip with his tongue or scratched his nose with his forefinger; but he was like an absent-minded man whose thoughts are half elsewhere, and who has to take a brief moment to register every question. There were none of the subtle human responses of sympathy that continually pass between two human beings as they converse. And when Niall tried to tune in to his thought waves, there was nothing there. It was an eerie feeling, like talking to a ghost.

The old man sighed. "Yes, it is true that I am a fairly crude device. When men were forced to leave the earth, computers had only been invented for two and a half centuries. No doubt men have now perfected computer holograms that are indistinguishable from real people."

"How can you read my thoughts?"

"The language circuits of your left brain work on simple wave patterns. When you think in words, the Steegmaster can detect them. But it cannot detect your feelings or intuitions. In that respect, it is far inferior to your own brain."

"I wish I could understand everything you say. What is a language circuit?"

"It is simpler to show you than to try to explain. Let us go back."

As he stood up, Steeg pushed back his chair with his legs. Niall was fascinated to observe the precision of his responses; there was nothing to indicate that he was bodiless.

Back in the picture gallery, the sun had risen to a point that indicated mid-morning.

"Is that the real sun?" Niall asked.

"No. If that were the real sun, you would see the spider city by its light. But no more questions. In a few hours, you will be able to answer them all for yourself. Please lie down again."

Niall positioned himself once more on the bed underneath the blue metal canopy; again, the light came on as soon as his body sank into its yielding surface. Then the enormous sense of peace and relaxation once more washed gently through his nervous system, bringing an upsurge of tremendous joy. But this time there was no desire to sleep. He was conscious of some point above his head, like an eye looking down from behind the opaque glass and conveying images directly into his brain. It was a strange process, not unlike dreaming. At the same time, a voice seemed to speak inside his chest, although it was not using human language; instead, it was evoking in him the insights and responses that language would have aroused.

When he closed his eyes, he saw the spider city spread out before him as he had first seen it from the gap in the hills: that city of immense square towers—which he now knew were called skyscrapers—with the great river dividing it into two. Then, as if he was rising vertically into the air, the city was below him. Moments later, he could see the sea, and the harbour with its great stone blocks. Then both the city and the harbour dwindled below him until they were reduced to one single point in a broad green plain. He could see the land on the other side of the ocean, and the red desert beyond the mountains. Somewhere there was the burrow, where his dead father lay. As soon as he tried to see it more clearly, the mental image became static and he was able to trace the contours of the great plateau, and of the great salt lake south of Dira. Then, once more, he was rising, so that he could see the lands to the south of the salt lake and to the north of the spider city. His speed increased until he could see the curve of the earth's surface, and the green lands below began to blend into a light blue, while the sea itself became darker. Soon he could see the earth as a furry ball, turning slowly in space. The stars looked enormous and brilliant, as if made of a kind of crystallised ice that was illuminated from inside. To his right, the sun was a ball of exploding radiance that hurt his eyes, so he had to look away. The moon was now a vast silver globe—it seemed strange to realise that it was a sphere when he had seen it all his life as a flat golden plate floating through the clouds. And although only part of its surface was illuminated by the sun, he could clearly see its darkened areas by the brilliant light of the stars.

Then they were out in space, up above the plane of the solar system, so far that the sun itself was hardly larger than an eyeball. One by one, Niall was made aware of the planets in their elliptical orbits: of Mercury, that tiny ball of red hot iron whose surface is as cracked as a wizened apple, of Venus, swathed in its atmosphere of sulphurous mist, of Mars with its frozen red deserts, of Jupiter, the vast red giant made of bubbling liquid, of the grey wanderer Saturn, whose immense bulk consists mainly of frozen hydrogen, and of Uranus, Neptune and Pluto, whose temperatures are so low that they are little more than floating balls of ice. Niall felt chilled and overawed by the sheer size of the solar system. From the orbit of its outermost planet, Pluto, the sun looked the size of a pea, while the earth was an almost invisible pinhead. Yet the nearest stars were still as far away from him as the earth's equator is from its polar caps.

When Niall's attention returned to the present, he realised with a shock that he had forgotten who he was. This experience had absorbed him so completely that his identity seemed slightly absurd. In the past, he had frequently "lost himself" in daydreams, or in stories told by his mother or grandfather. These had ignited his imagination; but compared with this experience, they seemed no more than a spark compared to a bonfire. It left him stunned and breathless, feeling like a man who has suddenly awakened from a dream. Immense forces were stirring inside him. He longed to ask a thousand questions, to be allowed to visit every planet in turn, then to voyage through space to other stars and solar systems. He experienced something like despair at the thought that knowledge was infinite and his own life so short.

As these thoughts disrupted his inner peace like an earthquake, the wordless voice inside him seemed to advise him to be patient. The negative emotions were dissolved away; instead, he experienced a consuming appetite for knowledge, a desire to devote the rest of his life to learning and understanding.

"Ask any questions you like," the old man's voice said. "The Steegmaster contains the sum of all human knowledge. It is for you to decide what you want to know."

"Could you tell me about the earth before the spiders came, and about the men who built this city?"

"For that we need to go back nearly five thousand million years, to the birth of the solar system . . . "

As he closed his eyes again, the voice was no longer coming from the old man but from inside him. Now he was watching a blinding explosion that seemed to fill all space, and that hurled great spirals of gas away from its centre like the arms of an octopus. The explosion seemed to go on forever, sending wave after wave of searing, destructive energy into space. Then, very slowly, it subsided, and its own gravity turned the initial explosion into an implosion. The remaining gases, sucked back together again, began to rotate in an immense whirlpool. Gradually, in the freezing cold of space, it lost its heat until the gases condensed into drops of liquid. Half a billion years later, these droplets had condensed into ten planets. Some, like Mercury, were too hot to retain an atmosphere; some like Mars, were too small and too cold. Only the earth, nearly a hundred million miles away from the sun, was neither too hot nor too cold.

The formation of the planet was as violent as its birth. Comets and fragments of planets crashed into it, churning it into a mass of boiling mud. It took two billion years for the earth to cool from a seething inferno into a planet with seas and continents. By then, it had shrunk to about a thousandth of its original size. And the sun had also been shrinking steadily, until it reached a point where nuclear reactions began and it turned from a dark globe into a dull red mass, then into a raging atomic furnace. Its ultra-violet rays penetrated the earth's thin atmosphere—mostly of hydrogen and ammonia—and caused violent electrical storms. And as the gases and water vapour were subjected to this bombardment, the first complex molecules began to form—the sugars and amino-acids. There also appeared a molecule called DNA—deoxyribonucleic acid—which had the peculiar property of duplicating itself. It was DNA that created the first form of life on earth—the bacteria. The bacteria possessed only one simple instinct—to gobble up the organic compounds floating around them in the warm seas, and so steal their energy. Life began as an energy-vampire.

At this early stage, life was almost destroyed by its own success. Bacteria flourished so abundantly that they had soon eaten up most of the organic compounds in the sea. Life would have vanished as quickly as it started if one of these bacteria had not discovered a new trick: manufacturing its own food by absorbing the energy of the sun. By this process—known as photosynthesis—the bacteria learned to make sugar from carbon dioxide and water. They absorbed the sunlight through a chemical called chlorophyll, and the chlorophyll gave these tiny organisms a green colour. Soon, the rocks around earth's continents—there were four immense continents at this time—were stained with a green, slimy substance, the first algae. And the blue-green algae drank the carbon dioxide from the earth's atmosphere and turned it back into oxygen.

Another immense period of time drifted past, during which the earth's atmosphere became increasingly rich in oxygen. Once more, life was in danger of destroying itself through its own success—for to plants, oxygen is a poison, and an earth that contained only plants would die from lack of carbon dioxide. But before this could happen, a new life form appeared—a form that could absorb oxygen and change it into carbon dioxide. These tiny blobs of swimming jelly were the first animals.

As Niall looked down on the earth of a billion years ago, he saw a peaceful and static planet whose warm seas lapped gently on the shores of the barren continents—or rather, on the shores of the barren continent, for the four continents had now drifted together to form one immense land mass known to geologists as Pangaea. On this placid globe, nothing ever changed. For, oddly enough, there was no death. These primitive amoebas and worms and algae shed their old cells and grew new ones, and went on living for ever.

And then, somehow, life invented death, and all the amazing complexities of evolution became possible. What happened is that these simple living creatures learned how to reproduce themselves, so the parent could die, and the young take over.

A creature that goes on living for millions of years falls into a lazy rhythm of existence. It knows how to survive, and that is enough. But when a new creature is born, it knows nothing whatever. It has to fight to establish a foothold. And it has to develop the power to *remember* what it had learned. An immortal creature has no need for memory; it learned the basic tricks of survival millions of years ago . . . A new-born creature has to pack its learning into a very short period, otherwise it will not survive. The ancient, immortal organisms were mere vegetables; the new life forms were fighters and learners.

And with the invention of death, history begins. These new organisms were no longer identical; they had individuality. And their individuality meant that they explored new environments, and so began to change in themselves. New types began to evolve, new species. Sometimes, an accidental change in the DNA—some careless piece of duplication that gave the creature an extra eye or a finger—made it better able to adapt to its environment than its brothers and sisters; so it survived while they died out. Blobs of jelly turned into worms and fishes and molluscs. And some of those fishes were so spectacularly successful there was no need for further change. The giant shark arrived on earth nearly four hundred million years ago, and his descendants resemble him in every particular.

But it is a basic law of life that, in some paradoxical sense, the less successful species are the most successful. For they go on struggling and evolving while the successful ones remain static. At roughly the same time the giant shark appeared on earth, certain fishes with large fleshy fins made a habit of struggling up onto the beach to escape their enemies and relax in the sunlight. They were not particularly well adapted to life out of water; if the tide went out, their fleshy fins were hardly powerful enough to enable them to struggle back to the sea. And their lungs found a diet of undiluted air painfully difficult to cope with—many of them lost consciousness and suffocated before they could regain the sea. Yet the land was so much safer than the sea—for it had no other living creatures—that these early amphibians preferred to risk exhaustion and death to taking their chance among the sharks. They became the first reptiles. And after another two hundred million years of evolution, the reptiles had become the lords of the earth. The plant-eating dinosaurs were the largest creatures the earth has ever known—the brontosaurus was often twenty-five yards long and weighed thirty tons. The meat-eating dinosaurs—like tyranosaurus—were the fiercest creatures the earth has ever known. And the flying dinosaurs—the archaeopteryx and the pterodactyl—became the most mobile creatures the earth had ever known. For a hundred and fifty million years, the dinosaurs dominated. And then they became the victims of their own success. Some great catastrophe—probably a giant meteor—ploughed into the earth sixty-five million years ago and threw up a cloud of steam that turned the atmosphere into a greenhouse. The temperature soared, and the plant-eating dinosaurs, with their huge bodies, died of excess heat. The flesh-eaters, which lived off the plant-eaters, died of starvation. And, for the first time, the warm-blooded animals had a chance to multiply and flourish. The death of the dinosaurs set the scene for the appearance of man.

Man's earliest mammalian ancestor was a rodent—a tiny tree shrew with a long tail and a flexible spine. Over ten million years or so ago, they developed a flexible thumb opposite their fingers to aid them in climbing trees. The shrew developed into a monkey. Ten million more years and the monkey had become an ape. And a mere five million years ago the chimpanzee developed into two new types of ape: the gorilla and the ape-man. And the ape-man arrived on earth in time for a twelve-million-year drought known as the Pliocene era. As the vegetation decreased, the ape-man came down from his trees to spend an increasing amount of time on the ground, digging for roots and worms. He began to develop his earliest and most interesting talent—walking upright on his hind limbs. And since he could no longer rely on the forest to provide him with food, he had to learn to generalise—to scratch some kind of a living from any environment—desert, woodland, mountains, frozen tundra. And in order to cope with these new problems, he developed the largest brain of any living creature.

When, about three million years ago, the weather changed, the ape-man had become the world's most adaptable animal. Suddenly there were lakes and rivers and vast plains of grass; and on these plains were herds of grass-eating animals. The ape-man had always been capable of cooperation with others of his kind, but there had been little opportunity for it in the drought of the Pliocene. Now cooperation became a necessity. A single man stood no chance against the mammoth, the cave bear, the woolly rhinoceros, the giant red deer and the sabre-toothed tiger; but a group of hunters, lying in ambush with spears and bone clubs, were a match for most animals. The upright posture gave man an immense advantage. And the skill required in hunting developed his brain at an incredible rate. The early ape Ramapithecus had a brain that weighed about four hundred grams. The brain of the hunter was half as big again. And in a mere two million years, *homo erectus* had a thousand-gram brain. Then, only a half million years ago, it increased its size yet again by fifty per cent. This remains the average brain size of modern man.

Homo erectus invented the hand axe for skinning animals, but in a million years he made no attempt to develop this simple tool—for example, to provide it with a handle and use it as a weapon. About three-quarters of a million years ago, a group of *homo eructus* arrived in Europe from Africa and Asia and evolved into *homo sapiens,* the species to which modern man belongs. This new type of man did not know how to make fire, but when lightning set the forests alight, he carefully preserved the fire and kept it burning year after year. He used it to set fire to the undergrowth and drive animals into traps or over clifftops; he also used it for cooking. The great ice ages came and he used the fire to keep warm in his caves. It may have been fire that produced the "brain explosion" of half a million years ago, for it obliged man to live in integrated societies and forced him to learn the disciplines of a social animal. A small tribe of twenty or thirty human beings can live as simply as a herd of cattle. But a group of a hundred or two hundred has to learn to organise itself. Laws and customs become necessary. Above all, he has to learn good manners. The primitive grunts that had once served to communicate had to evolve into a more sophisticated language.

There were two main sub-species of human beings about a hundred and twenty thousand years ago. One looked like modern man and was found mainly in Africa. The other, Neanderthal man, was more primitive and ape-like, yet in many ways, just as intelligent. He invented the bow and arrow, which meant that hunters could kill their prey from a distance. His women decorated themselves with red ochre. Moreover, he worshipped the sun and believed in an afterlife—or at least, we can make this assumption from the fact that he manufactured stone spheres and discs and buried his dead with some form of ritual involving flowers. For more than fifty thousand years, Neanderthal man was the dominant human species. And then, suddenly, he disappeared. And his disappearance corresponds with the sudden rise of his more "human" brother, Cro-Magnon man. It seems probable that our ancestors wiped out their Neanderthal rivals between thirty and forty thousand years ago and took over the continent of Europe for themselves.

Compared to Neanderthal men, Cro-Magnon men were supermen. They learned to communicate by speaking in sentences instead of grunts. Their priests—or shamans—used a kind of magic to aid the hunters, drawing pictures of their prey on the walls of caves and performing certain rituals to induce them to walk into the hunter's ambush. They even developed the first form of writing, scratching marks on bone to enable them to predict the phases of the moon and the march of the seasons. They learned to make boats to cross rivers, and were soon using them to cross the seas. Now they could speak, men who lived hundreds of miles apart could trade with one another, exchanging flints, pottery and animal skins. They learned to domesticate animals—the wolf (which became the dog), the horse, the goat, and to breed cattle and sheep. About ten thousand years ago, they began to develop agriculture, learning to grow wheat and barley. And it was not long after this that they built the first walled cities, and man embarked on a new stage of his evolution.

"So you see, these early farmers had reached roughly the same stage as the men of today. The spiders have put back the clock of human evolution by ten thousand years."

Niall opened his eyes, unsure of whether it was Steeg who had spoken; but the old man was nowhere to be seen.

It was like waking from a very deep sleep; the room in which he was lying looked totally strange. Then he noticed that the sun was shining through the windows on the other side of the gallery; it was already late afternoon. He calculated that he had been lying there for eight hours. The sense of deep relaxation was the effect of the peace machine; by removing all the physical tensions that normally accumulate during prolonged mental activity, it enabled his mind to remain focused on the dream-like panorama that passed before his inner vision.

At the suggestion of some inner prompting, he made his way back to the food machine and ate a bowl of soup and an apple—noticing only as he swallowed the last mouthful that the apple had no core. He was uninterested in the food; all his being was directed to trying to absorb all he had learned and to grasp its implications.

Half an hour later, still damp from a shower—he had coped with the complexities of the bathroom with the mechanical certainty of a sleepwalker—he returned to the peace machine and lay down under its canopy, closing his eyes.

Without any transition, he found himself standing in a landscape that seemed vaguely familiar. This time, he was actually present, with no sense of his body lying on its couch. He was standing on the seashore looking towards a range of hills in the distance. There were many shrubs and palm trees, and the dry soil had a covering of marram grass. Half a mile away was a walled city. Its buildings were of baked mud, and the wall that surrounded it was a mixture of baked mud and stone. As he stared at the line of hills, he suddenly recognised the place. This was the great salt lake of Dira, and the city stood on the site of the ruined city where Niall had killed the spider.

The voice said: "Why do you suppose the city has a wall?"

"For protection against wild animals?"

"No. For protection against other men. These men who created civilisation had also learned that it is easier to steal your neighbour's corn and cattle than to raise your own. That is why they needed walls. Crime and civilisation were born at the same time."

The comment troubled Niall; it seemed somehow illogical. Civilisation seemed momentous and significant, man's greatest single step towards control over his own life. By comparison crime seemed trivial and insignificant. Why was the voice speaking about them as if they were equally important?

"Because crime is far more important than you realise—not in itself, but as a symptom of mankind's greatest problem. Think of what it meant for men to live in cities. It was no longer necessary for every man to be a hunter or a farmer, and for every woman to be a mother and a housekeeper. Because there were so many people living together, each one could perform a different task. There were builders and farmers and weavers and toolmakers and priests. Each one had to narrow down his sights to a single specialised job. You have spent your life in the desert, struggling to find food and drink. Therefore you regarded Kazak's city as a kind of paradise. But what about the people who had been living there all their lives? Did they regard it as a paradise?"

"No."

"Why not?"

"Because they were used to it."

"Quite. And that soon became the problem of these early city dwellers. It had taken man two hundred million years to evolve from a tree shrew, and he often came close to extinction. He had battled against every kind of danger and natural catastrophe just to stay alive. And then, in the mere blink of an eyelid, he had comfort and security . . . and specialisation. It happened much too fast. He couldn't change the habits of millions of years in a single lifetime. So he kept reverting back to his older self—the hunter-warrior. That is why he went to war with his neighbours. It made him feel alive again."

"But wasn't he simply destroying everything he had fought for?"

"No. Because the need for comfort and security is even stronger than the need for excitement and adventure. We want security first, *then* adventure—not the other way round. Besides, mere war and excitement failed to satisfy his most powerful appetite—his intelligence. It was a deeper urge than the craving for excitement that led him to invent the hoe and the plough, the wheel and the sail . . ."

The words faded, and once again Niall found himself watching an inner-panorama of history and understanding it without the need for explanations. He saw the building of the first cities in Mesopotamia and Egypt and China, the rise of the warrior kings, the construction of stone temples and pyramids, the discovery of bronze, then of iron. He witnessed the rise and fall of empires: the Sumerians, the Egyptians, the Minoans, the Chaldeans and the Assyrians. He also witnessed cruelties that left him feeling shaken and physically sick. He was spared nothing of the destruction of cities and the torture and murder of their inhabitants. The steles of the Assyrians came to life, and he watched them flogging their prisoners, beheading them, burning them alive and impaling them on stakes. It made him burn with rage, and he watched the downfall and extinction of the Assyrian warlords with malicious satisfaction. But when it was over, he felt tainted by his own anger and hatred.

Then the scene changed to ancient Greece, and his disgust vanished as he witnessed the story of the rise of Hellenic civilisation, the birth of democracy and philosophy, the invention of the drama, the discovery of geometry and experimental science. Once again he experienced that sense of enormous excitement at the widening of man's evolutionary horizons, and a sense of pride at belonging to the human species.

In spite of the soothing effects of the peace machine, the strain of absorbing so much knowledge was exhausting. While he was watching the story of the war between Athens and Sparta, the pictures began to blend together, and then dissolved into a dream. He woke a few hours later to find himself in darkness, and covered with a blanket. Through the window, he could see the dome of the cathedral outlined against the stars. And when he woke again it was already mid-morning, and he could hear the cry of the boatmen, and the vendors in the market place. Once again, he found the food machine and went through the automatic process of eating and drinking; food and drink seemed unimportant in comparison with his craving to learn the remainder of the story of mankind. Then he hurried back and lay down once more under the frosted glass screen.

This time, the dream showed him the story of ancient Rome. He witnessed the age of democratic government, the wars against Carthage, the rise of the dictator emperors: Marius and Sulla, Julius Caesar, Augustus, Tiberius, Caligula, Claudius, Nero. Once again, he was appalled and morbidly fascinated by this endless tale of bloodshed and stupidity. The story of the birth of Christianity engendered a mood of hope; this doctrine of love and universal brotherhood seemed the most promising development since the birth of civilisation. The history of the Church's rise to power under the emperor Constantine made him realise that his optimism had been premature. These Christians showed even less tolerance of their religious opponents than the Romans had done; they even murdered one another over obscure doctrinal points. After witnessing the downfall of Rome under the onslaught of the barbarians, Niall experienced a certain weary resignation. As the picture faded and he again became conscious of his surroundings, he asked:

"Does it go on like this? Is all human history so depressing?"

The voice inside him said: "Not entirely. The next thousand years are depressing because the Church tried to maintain its grip on the minds of men and killed anyone who tried to think for himself. But all that began to change at about the time Brunelleschi built the dome of that cathedral out there." Niall sat up, massaging his eyes. "The change began with a series of great wars called the Crusades, when men began to travel instead of staying in the same place all the time. That broadened their minds, and they built ships and began to explore the world. Then a man called John Gooseflesh invented printing, and someone else learned how to make cheap paper, and suddenly there were millions of books. Then the Church began to lose the battle to prevent people from thinking for themselves . . ."

Niall's fatigue suddenly vanished; he lay down again and closed his eyes.

"Show me."

This new installment of the tale was the most absorbing so far. He witnessed the story of the Reformation, then how an amateur astronomer named Copernicus realised that the earth travelled round the sun. He saw the invention of the telescope and the great battle between Galileo and Pope Paul V about whether the earth was really the centre of the universe. He witnessed the discoveries of Sir Isaac Newton and the foundation of the Royal Society, and watched with delight as the voice of the Age of Reason refused to be silenced by the threats of the Church. He began to feel that at last humanity had discovered the secret of peace and greatness. He even applauded the storming of the Bastile and the execution of Louis XVI—for surely the execution of a few tyrants was excusable in the name of freedom and the brotherhood of man?

The nineteenth century seemed to justify his excitement. With its invention of the railway, the steamship, the telegraph, electric light, it seemed to promise the emergence of a new kind of man. But even as these thoughts filled him with optimism—and perhaps as a response to his optimism—the scene changed to a panorama of nineteenth-century wars and revolutions: the Napoleonic wars, the revolutions of 1848, the Crimean war, the Indian mutiny, the American Civil war, the Franco—Prussian war, the Russo—Turkish war, and once again he felt himself slipping into depression. It seemed incredible that his own species should be capable of so much greatness and so much stupidity. But as he stirred restively, the voice said:

"Be patient for a while. There are still interesting developments to come."

So Niall closed his eyes again, and tried to suspend his judgement as he witnessed the history of the twentieth century: the Great War, the Russian revolution, the rise of the Fascists and the Nazis, the Sino—Japanese war, the Second World War, the invention of the atomic and hydrogen bombs, and the uneasy armed peace that these brought about. The scale of human achievement continued to excite him: the aeroplane, radio and television, the computer, the exploration of space. But by now he had become aware of the basic pattern, and had begun to fear that nothing could change it. It seemed depressingly obvious that man had grown into an intellectual giant while remaining an emotional pygmy.

The voice read his thoughts. "Yes, it is true that the history of the human race seems to point towards catastrophe. But that is because I am forced to oversimplify. If you could spend six months here, studying everything in more detail, you would find more cause for hope. Man really has remarkable powers of adaptation."

"But did they go on behaving so stupidly until the comet forced them to leave the earth?"

"For some time, yes. Although atomic weapons forced them to stop fighting world wars, they made up for it with hundreds of minor wars. And meanwhile, their crime rate became so appalling that people were forced to turn their houses into fortresses. In spite of all attempts to prevent it, the world's population continued to rise until the cities were like overcrowded ant hills where it was dangerous to walk the streets. Early in the twenty-first century, they invented a weapon that made war more fascinating and devastating than ever—the Reaper. It was a kind of machine-gun that fired a beam of atomic energy, so that it could be used to cut down a tree or demolish a whole street full of houses. Man found it impossible to resist using anything so magnificently destructive; it became the favourite weapon of terrorists—people who try to achieve their political ends through violence—and governments found it practically impossible to control them.

"And then, in the middle of the twenty-first century, two doctors—a great physiologist and a great psychologist—built the first peace machine. This was one of the most important inventions in the history of the human race. Suddenly, man had a simple method of releasing all the tensions that had made him so destructive. In the past, they had invented various drugs that had a similar effect, but men became addicted to them and wasted their lives. The peace machine was not addictive—it simply left them relaxed and full of energy and courage. Mental illness almost disappeared. So did violent crime. Wars also became increasingly rare. For a while, men congratulated themselves on having solved their greatest problem, and the two scientists—Chater and Takahashi—were regarded almost as saints—Takahashi became president of the federated Afro—European states. The population rate also began to fall, so that by the year 2100 there were less human beings on earth than in 1900.

"Yet by that time it had become clear that the greatest of all problems remained. Man had not solved the secret of happiness. In spite of the low crime rate and the freedom from stress, men still felt strangely unfulfilled. They felt that life should be something more than a peaceful, pleasant routine, and that man needed new worlds to conquer. And since they knew there were no such worlds in their own solar system, they began to experiment with space craft in an effort to reach the stars. They had received signals from space that told them there was intelligent life in the star cluster called Alpha Centauri. But even the light from Centauri takes five years to reach the earth. Their fastest space craft would take centuries to reach the nearest star. They decided that the answer was to build space craft that were like miniature planets, containing gardens and rivers—even mountains. The first of these was launched in the year 2100 and set out for the planetary system of Proxima Centauri. Twenty years later, it was overtaken by the first of a new type of space craft with laser drive—an energy that enabled them to reach half the speed of light. The first craft to reach the Centauri system arrived in the year 2130 and established a small colony called New Earth. But most of its inhabitants became homesick and spent another ten years returning.

"Back on earth, the situation remained much as before. The crime rate had started to rise again, because people were beginning to commit crimes out of boredom. But at least men were intelligent enough to understand the nature of the problem. It was simply that man had evolved much too fast. It had taken him more than a million years to change from a cave dweller into a city dweller, but a mere seven thousand years—less than three hundred generations—to change from a city dweller into a space explorer. Even his body was not ready for the change. It was made for hard work and effort, not for sitting in office chairs. All his instincts were directed towards struggle, and he felt suffocated by his comfortable, peaceful civilisation. Men even began to look back nostalgically on the days when war and crime made life more dangerous. A famous biologist wrote a book asserting that the human race would finally die of boredom.

"At that point men suddenly learned that life was in danger of being destroyed by a radioactive comet. It was like a great awakening. Now they had one single aim—to avert the catastrophe. At first they thought of destroying the comet, or trying to divert it, but it was simply too big—fifty thousand miles in diameter. When it became obvious that the collision was inevitable, and that it would occur in less than five years, they began to devote their immense technical resources to building more than a thousand giant space transports. Other scientists began a race to find ways of making human beings immune to radioactivity, by studying the scorpions who are able to absorb hundreds of times as much radiation as animals. They thought they had probably discovered the solution, but few human beings were willing to try it. In the year 2175, the earth was finally evacuated. Six weeks later, the comet passed close to earth and brushed it with its tail. It destroyed nine-tenths of all animal life, including most of the human beings who stayed behind.

"The last of the space transports left the solar system a few weeks later. An astronomer on board took the last photographs of the comet as it swung around the sun and headed out into space. And he saw something that baffled him. The tail of a comet always points away from the sun, because it is created by the pressure of sunlight on the light gases. Yet as Opik began to leave the solar system, its tail was apparently still pointing backwards. Most scientists refused to accept the evidence of the photographs, because they said it was impossible. But a few began to wonder whether the collision between the comet and the earth was really the million to one chance they had all supposed . . .

"This tower, and forty-nine more like it, were built in various parts of the earth. This was the first to be built. It was originally intended to be a museum—or time capsule, as they called it—containing the sum of all human knowledge. It is also designed to gather information about what happened on earth after the great exodus."

"But how can you gather information without leaving the tower?"

"From the minds of human beings. Thought-reading machines were invented late in the twenty-first century, as a by-product of research into sleep-learning. When men learned how to feed knowledge directly into the human memory circuits, they also discovered how to decipher what was already stored in those circuits."

Niall found the thought disquieting. "So you can read everything that goes on in my mind?"

"No. I said thought-reading machines, not mind-reading machines. Your thoughts are only the topmost layer of your mind. They operate on a series of coded signals which can be detected like radio waves. A powerful thought-reading machine can decipher most of the contents of your long-term memory. But it has no power to detect your feelings or intuitions—or the decisions of your will. We collect most of our information from the brains of human beings while they are asleep."

"But what do you want if *for*?"

"So the men of New Earth can stay in touch with what is happening on earth."

Niall's heart leapt. "You are able to speak to them?"

"All the information gathered by the Steegmaster is transmitted direct to New Earth."

"So they already know about me?"

"Not yet. It takes five years for the radio signals to reach them."

"But they know about the spiders?"

"Of course."

Niall said eagerly: "Do you think they might come back to earth and help us fight them?"

"No. Why should they?"

The bluntness startled and dismayed him. He answered lamely: "Because . . . because they are human beings too."

"True. But it would take them ten years to reach the earth, even after they had received your message. Why should they go to so much trouble to help you when you could help yourself?"

The answer rekindled his feeling of hope. "Do you believe we *could* do it ourselves?"

"If you cannot, then you do not deserve to be free. The law of life is the survival of the fittest. If you cannot defeat the spiders, then you are not fit to survive, and they would deserve to remain the masters of the earth."

This made Niall thoughtful. He said finally: "When I first came here, you promised you would show me how to defeat the spiders. Could you do that?"

"I could."

"But will you?"

"I am afraid it is not permitted."

Niall's heart sank. "Why not?"

There was a pause, then the voice said: "I will make a bargain with you. If you can tell *me* why not, then I will try to help you."

Niall shook his head in bewilderment. "Is it some kind of riddle?"

"No. Just a bargain."

"But . . . how long can I have to think about it?"

"As far as I am concerned, it is a matter of indifference. But I would not advise you to take too long."

"Why not?"

"Because the longer you stay, the more difficult you will find it to escape. The spiders are still unaware that you are missing. When they find out, it will not take them long to guess where you are hiding. When that happens, there will be an army of spiders to prevent you leaving the tower."

"But how will they guess where I am?"

"You were seen coming towards the tower—have you forgotten?"

Niall remembered the wolf spiders who had been guarding the headquarters of the Death Lord.

"Why haven't they raised the alarm?"

"Because no one knows you are missing yet."

Niall found himself automatically looking out of the window; it was frustrating to see the citizens of Florence going placidly about their business. He asked:

"Do you know what is happening to my mother and brother?"

"Yes."

"Can you tell me?"

The voice said: "Close your eyes."

As soon as Niall's eyelids closed, he found himself in Kazak's palace. There was nothing dreamlike about the experience. He was standing in a corner of the room in which he had last spoken to Kazak. There were four people in the room: Kazak, Veig, his mother and the black-clad guard who had locked him up. The woman was standing to attention, staring straight in front of her. Siris was seated on a pile of cushions; her face looked set and exhausted. The king was standing with his back to the room, looking out of the window. Veig was also standing; Niall thought he looked unhappy and unsure of himself.

"We know he must be hiding somewhere in this city," Kazak said. "If you want to see him alive again, we have to find him before the spiders do."

Veig shook his head. "If we could understand why he ran away . . ."

Kazak said irritably: "I've told you, I don't know. It was a stupid thing to do. Everything seemed to be going so well . . ."

Veig said: "I think he's trying to get back to the nursery."

Siris gave a startled cry; she was staring at Niall. It made Kazak start convulsively. He said angrily: "What the devil are you . . ." Then he also saw Niall. His face expressed astonishment and relief.

"Thank God for that! Where on earth have you been?"

When Niall tried to reply, he found he had no voice. It was a nightmarish sensation; his lips moved, but no sound came out. Then he felt the scene fading. When he opened his eyes, he was still standing by the open window, looking down at the Arno. The old man was standing a few feet away, regarding him with an ironic smile. The whole experience had taken only a few seconds.

He asked: "What happened?"

"You broke the contact."

Niall was feeling so dizzy that he had to sit down on the nearest bench. His heart was pounding violently, and perspiration was running down his face. For a moment he thought he was about to faint. Then the sickness passed, and his vision cleared. He felt very tired.

"They saw me."

"Your mother saw you. So did Kazak."

"Not the other two?" It all happened so quickly that he had not noticed.

"No."

He buried his face in his hands; it made him feel better.

"Why is my head so strange?"

"You tried to speak, and drained all your psychic energy . . ."

"But they *saw* me. I was there."

"They saw you with their minds, not their eyes."

After a minute, his heart ceased to pound. His throat felt dry and parched.

"I'm going to get a drink."

He made his way along the corridor to the food machine. It was no surprise to find Steeg there already, seated at the table by the window. Niall pressed one of the "drink" buttons at random; half a minute later, a glass of cold orange juice emerged from the chute; tiny petals of orange were floating on its surface. Niall drank it thirstily. He sat down opposite the old man. He asked:

"What will happen now?"

"Now Kazak will be more determined than ever to find you. He believes you possess supernatural powers. He cannot afford to lose you."

The memory of his mother's pale face filled Niall with a sense of guilt. For a moment he contemplated returning to Kazak's palace.

Steeg shook his head. "That would be stupid. This time they would never let you out of their sight."

Niall stared sombrely out of the window. "Where can I go?"

The old man smiled. "First, you must complete your side of the bargain."

"The riddle?"

"Not a riddle. A simple question."

Niall buried his face in his hands, but it did nothing to clarify his thoughts.

"You want me to tell you . . . why you can't help me to destroy the spiders."

"Not quite. You asked me if I could tell you how to defeat the spiders. I told you that it was not permitted. But I didn't refuse to *help* you."

"But you want me to think it out for myself?"

He nodded. "You are beginning to understand."

Niall said slowly: "You can't tell me how to destroy the spiders . . . because"—he groped for words—"because that would be too easy. Men have to find their own freedom . . . or they won't appreciate what it is to be free." He looked at the old man. "Is that the answer to your riddle?"

"It is a part of the answer."

Niall shook his head; his brain still felt weary. "I can't think of any more."

"Then it will serve for the time being."

Niall asked quickly: "Then you'll help me?"

"First of all, let me ask you another question. Why do you want to destroy the spiders?"

"Because they are our enemies."

"But they are not my enemy. I want to know why you think they deserve to be destroyed and man deserves to survive. Is man so much better than the spiders?"

The question troubled Niall; he suspected a logical trap. He said finally: "Men built this city, and the spiders never built cities. They live in the cities left behind by men."

"But they are masters of the earth. Does that not prove they are superior to men?"

"No. They have stronger wills, that's all. That doesn't make them better."

"Why not?"

Niall thought about it and shook his head. "I can't explain. But I *feel* it's true."

The old man said gently: "If you intend to fight the spiders, you need to *know* why it is true."

"Can you tell me?"

"I can do better than that. I can show you. Come."

Niall followed him out of the room, down the corridor and back into the gallery. He was expecting to be taken to the peace machine. But the old man went past it and stepped into the white column. Niall followed. He felt himself rising. When he stepped forward again, they were in the room at the top of the tower with the view over the city. It seemed strange to see it again. The illusion of Florence had been so complete that he felt as though he had been away. The sun was close to the western horizon.

Steeg pointed to the black leather couch. "Lie down there."

Beside the couch on a table of black glass lay a device made of curved strips of metal: it might have been a rudimentary hat. It was connected to the Steegmaster by a length of wire.

"Place it on your head," Steeg said.

His order was accompanied by a mental image. Niall did as he was told. Small felt-covered pads pressed against his forehead and his temples.

"Lie down comfortably and place your head on the pillow. Are you ready?"

Niall nodded. He experienced a faint electrical tingle where the pads touched his skin. He closed his eyes.

He had been expecting to receive some kind of mental image, perhaps accompanied by a wordless flow of insight. In fact, the electrical tingling merely increased until it tickled the skin. This was accompanied by a pleasant sensation as if he had become bodiless and was floating free, like a balloon. The tingling sensation was now flowing from his head to his feet, and the pleasure became steadily more intense. He was completely unprepared for anything so inexpressibly delightful; the tingling seemed to turn into a kind of white light that suffused his whole body as if he had become transparent. It was not unlike the pleasure he had experienced as he pressed Merlew's body against his, but raised to a far higher degree.

Quite suddenly, it seemed as if a higher note of intensity sounded inside the white light, a note that was itself an intenser form of light. It rose higher and higher, and the light became as blinding as the sun at midday. All this was the prelude to an experience that lasted for perhaps five seconds.

So far, he had accepted all that had happened passively, with immense gratitude. But a point came where he became aware that these sensations were not being imposed upon him from outside. They were only a reflection of something that was happening inside. It was as if the sun were rising from below some horizon of his inner being. And then, for a few seconds, there was a sensation of raw power—a tremendous, overwhelming power rising from his own depths. It was accompanied by an insight that, for some reason made him want to laugh. The tower, the Steegmaster, the old man, even the spiders, all seemed a tremendous joke. And he, Niall, was also a joke, for he was aware that Niall was an impostor. In fact, he was an absurdity, for the truth was that he did not really exist.

Then the light faded, the sense of power diminished until it became merely a sense of pleasure, and he felt as if he was being lowered gently onto a beach by some powerful receding wave. Yet the insight remained. He knew now that the power came from inside himself.

The pads that pressed against his skin were no longer tingling. The whole room seemed transformed. He was looking at it as if he had created it. Nothing in it seemed strange or alien.

He remained perfectly still for several minutes, listening

to a diminishing echo of the sound that had carried him outside his personality. Then he sighed deeply and removed the device from his head, replacing it on the table. He felt very languid and tired, but totally serene.

The old man was no longer there but the voice inside his chest said: "Now you understand."

There was no point in replying. For the first time, he grasped clearly that the voice was merely the voice of a machine, programmed to respond to his own questions. He had known this before, yet because the machine behaved and sounded like a person, some deeper level of his mind had refused to accept it. Now he knew it was true.

For the moment, he wanted to lie still and absorb what he had just learned.

The prime fact was power.

Yet although this was so simple and obvious, it was also bewildering. The source of power was inside him. He used it every time he raised his hand or lowered his eyelids. Yet it was also strong enough to change the universe. Why did the men know so little about their inner power? Why did they make so little use of it? The answer was now clear. Because in order to make use of this power, man has to *summon* it. And to do this, he has to descend inside himself, and contract his mind to a point. But the process of falling asleep begins in the same way, with that withdrawal from the physical world and descent into the mind. So man seldom becomes aware of the power because he usually falls asleep before he reaches it . . .

Niall contracted his forehead, summoning all his energy in an act of concentration. He immediately experienced a brief flash of power. It was pale and feeble compared to the intensity of a few moments ago; but this was unimportant.

What was important was that he *could* induce it—no matter how dimly—by an act of will.

And now he could understand why the spiders had never progressed beyond a certain point. Throughout millions of years of their evolution, they had remained passive. This had enabled them to grasp an important secret—a secret unknown to men: that will-power is a physical force. Man had never discovered this because he was too busy using his brain and muscles—the instruments of his will. When a spider lured a fly into its web by the force of its will, it knew that force can be exerted without the use of any physical intermediary. So when the spiders became giants, they developed a giant will-power.

Yet even this was a step in the wrong direction. They learned to use the will as men learned to use their muscles; to make reality do their bidding. They directed it *outward*, towards other creatures. But because they had never learned to make active use of their brains, they failed to ask themselves about the source of this power. So they remained unaware of the immense power that lay hidden deep inside themselves. That was why they would be superseded my men. That was why they *knew* they would be superseded. That was why the Spider Lord was afraid of men.

He crossed to the transparent wall that faced north. On the other side of the lawn that surrounded the tower, the broad avenue continued in a straight line for perhaps another half mile. Beyond that, between half-ruined buildings, he could glimpse the river. Since the avenue appeared to continue without a break, it was clear there must be a bridge.

He asked: "Do you have a plan of the spider city?"

The room was immediately plunged into darkness as its walls became opaque. On the wall facing Niall, projected as if by a beam of light, there appeared an enormous map whose buildings were drawn in perspective, as if photographed at an angle from the air. The city, he could now see, had been designed in the form of a circle, with the great main avenue running from north to south, and the river serving as its east-west diameter. The women's quarters occupied the south-western segment, with the central dividing wall running far beyond the city's southern limit.

By far the largest section was the semicircle to the north of the river. This was labelled "Slave quarter," and the foreshortened drawings revealed that many of its buildings were ruins. Like the southern section, this also contained a large central square, occupied by a domed building surrounded by lawns.

Niall asked: "What is this?"

"It was once the city's administrative centre—the City Hall. Now it is used as a silk factory."

"For spider balloons?"

"For that and other purposes."

"Are the balloons made here?"

"No. The silk is transported to the city of the bombardier beetles, five miles to the north."

"Why not here?"

"Because the servants of the spiders lack the manual dexterity. Balloon making is a highly skilled job, and the servants of the beetles are more intelligent and more skilful."

"If the spiders are afraid of human intelligence, why do they allow the beetles to keep intelligent servants?"

"They have no choice. The beetles are immune from spider poison, and they can be dangerous when aroused."

"But why do the beetles want intelligent servants?"

"Because, unlike the spiders, they are fascinated by human achievement. They are also fascinated by human destructiveness. It is, you see, an evolutionary heritage.

They have always defended themselves by producing explosions—therefore, to them, explosions are beautiful. The chief business of their servants is to devise tremendous explosions. To do this, they need a fairly high degree of intelligence."

"That must worry the spiders."

"It did before the beetles and spiders reached an agreement. Now they operate a slave-exchange system. Intelligent beetle menservants are exchanged for attractive females from the spider city."

"Doesn't that anger the servants of the beetles—to see their men sold into slavery?"

"No. They are glad to have a choice of beautiful women. Besides, the servants of the beetles regard it is an enviable job—they are used for breeding."

Niall studied the map for a long time.

"Where would be the best place for me to hide?"

"Anywhere in the slave quarter. They would accept your presence without question."

"But are there no spiders there?"

"Many. But to them, one human being looks exactly like another. You only need to observe a reasonable degree of caution."

Niall suddenly experienced a pang of dread. Inside this tower, he was comfortable and safe. Now he was about to venture into unknown dangers, he experienced a child's overwhelming craving for peace and security. All the knowledge and insight he had acquired during the past two days seemed unimportant. For a moment, he felt something like despair.

The Steegmaster seemed unaware of this inner conflict. The voice said: "Before you leave, it would be advisable to commit the plan to memory."

"That would take a long time." He tried to keep the weariness out of his voice.

"Not as long as you think. Look in the cabinet beside the Steegmaster."

Niall opened the door of the grey metal cabinet and found himself looking at his own face. Its rear wall consisted of a mirror. Meeting his own eyes, he could see the misery and uncertainty reflected in them.

Hanging over the mirror, suspended on a tiny gold hook, there was a fine metal chain on the end of which was a small circular disc slightly more than an inch in diameter.

The voice said: "Take it and hang it around you neck. It is a thought mirror."

Niall unhooked it and looked at it carefully. The disc was slightly concave, and of a brown-gold colour. Now he looked more closely, he could see that it was not an exact circle; the shape was closer to a diamond with curved sides. The surface looked too dull to be a mirror; his face, golden and distorted, looked back at him as if through a cloud of mist.

As he hung it round his neck, the voice said: "No, the other way."

He turned it round so that the concave surfaced lay against his chest, resting slightly above the solar plexus. He immediately experienced a peculiar and indescribable sensation, as if some shock had caused his heart to contract. His eyes once again met his reflection in the mirror and he saw that the uncertainty had vanished.

The voice said: "The thought mirror was perfected by an ancient civilisation called the Aztecs; their shamans used it in meditation before performing a human sacrifice. The secret was rediscovered by paranormal researchers in the late twentieth century. It has the power to coordinate mental vibrations from the brain, the heart and the solar plexus. Now try to memorise the map."

Niall stared intently at the map. To his surprise, it no longer cost him a mental effort to grasp it as a whole. It was as if his powers of concentration were somehow aided and amplified by the mirror hanging on his chest. Five minutes earlier, the map had seemed too complicated and undigestible; now, suddenly, it was as if his mind was absorbing it hungrily, as his stomach might absorb food. In less than a minute, he knew it by heart.

He asked: "What is the Fortress?"

"It used to be the main barracks of this city. A barracks is a building that houses soldiers."

"And what is an arsenal?"

"A place where weapons are kept."

He pointed to the map. "Is the bridge guarded?"

"Yes. Last week, one of the commanders was caught as she tried to wade across—she wanted to get to the nursery to see her baby. Now wolf spiders guard both ends."

"What happened to her?"

"She was publicly executed and eaten."

"Is there any other point where it is possible to cross the river?"

"The bridge is still the best. The river is at its shallowest there."

"When would be the best time to attempt it?"

"At dawn, when the guard is changed."

Niall studied the map again. It would obviously be suicidal to try and approach the bridge down the main avenue. But the map showed flights of steps descending to the river at intervals of about half a mile along its embankment. If Niall could gain access to the river near the wall that divided the city, it should be possible to make his way to the bridge along the lower bank.

"Where should I look for shelter in the slave quarter?" he asked.

"Many of the buildings have lost their upper storeys. The spiders prefer not to use these for web-building. You would be safest in one of those."

Niall experienced a twinge of pain behind his eyes; when he massaged his cheeks and forehead with his hands, it went away.

The voice said: "The pain is due to the thought mirror." "You are not accustomed to using it, and unless you keep your attention concentrated, it will cause headaches. When that happens, turn it round the other way."

Niall turned the mirror so that it faced away from his chest. As soon as he did this, the sense of strain vanished. But he observed that he now felt curiously fatigued. The blood tingled in his cheeks. He lay down on the couch and closed his eyes. A pleasant drowsiness began to steal over him.

The voice said: "It would not be advisable to sleep now. The Spider Lord has just sent a message to Kazak, asking him to bring you to his presence. When Kazak admits you have gone, every spider in the city will be searching for you."

Niall sat up, his fatigue vanishing instantly. Once again, he had to control the fear that trickled into his bloodstream. He had to keep his voice steady as he asked.

"What will he do to Kazak?"

"Nothing. The Spider Lord is a realist. But you must leave now."

"Yes." An effort of concentration subdued his fear and renewed his determination. "Shall I be able to keep in touch with you?"

"Yes. Through the telescopic rod. It is attuned to the thought pattern of the Steegmaster. But use it sparingly.

Many of the spiders will be able to detect its energies. So whenever you use it, you will be in danger of discovery."

The old man suddenly appeared, standing by the white column. "Before you leave, I would advise you to eat. You have a long night before you."

"I don't feel like eating." His appetite had vanished.

"Then take food with you. You must also change into the uniform of the slaves. Follow me. There is now no time to lose."

Niall stepped into the column and felt himself descending; this time the feather-like sensation was unpleasant, underlining his nervous tension.

They were in the room with the white curved walls. On one of the stools—the one that Niall had mistaken for a weed-covered rock on the seashore—lay the telescopic rod and the coarse grey uniform of a slave. As he slipped it on over his own clothes, his nose wrinkled in disgust; it smelt of stale sweat.

Unlike his own garments, the slave uniform had two wide pockets. There was something in both of them. He investigated and found that one contained a small wooden box. In the other was a light grey tube, almost six inches long and an inch in diameter. In the box, under a layer of cotton wool, were a number of tiny brown tablets. The old man said:

"These are food tablets—a type developed by men to sustain them on long journeys in space."

"And this?"

"A lightweight garment, also developed for use in space. Touch the disc at the end."

When Niall pressed the end of the tube with his thumb, it elongated to twice its length, then unrolled. It was a baggy garment of dull metallic grey, and looked big enough for a man twice Niall's size. He asked:

"Is this necessary?"

"Take it. You may be grateful for it. When you press the end it will re-fold itself." Niall watched with amusement as it converted itself into a neat grey tube, and was surprised that it did this so silently without any of the rustling noise he would have expected.

"Now go, otherwise all the preparation will have been wasted."

He vanished. Niall felt disconcerted by the abruptness of the leavetaking, but it emphasised the sense of urgency.

As soon as he picked up the metal rod, he experienced a tingling sensation in his fingers; when he reached out and touched the wall with its end, his legs felt weak and he was overcome by sudden dizziness. He stepped forward and felt again as if he had fallen into whirlpool. For a moment there was acute nausea; then his senses cleared and he was standing on the grass outside the tower.